Lancer; Hero of the West

"The Prescott Affair"

A Novel

by

Bob Brill

I0458202

ISBN: 978-0-578-14024-7

For my Dad whose love of westerns grew into my love of Westerns.

Thank you to Roselle, who is a wonderful and dedicated book editor and who also works cheap; my daughter Julia, who is the best graphic artist I've ever met; to Cynthia Menck, who, at Sylmar High School in the early 1970's, taught me to be bold and step forward; and to my beautiful wife, Paula, who inspires me every day of my existence.

Cover design: Julia Chandrasekaran, Designer*Friendly.

FORWARD

My love of Westerns and the West in general
stems from my father, who told me he devoured
every Zane Grey novel he could get his hands on.
The Saturday afternoon matinee in Pittsburgh was
a refuge for him and his brothers, especially when
it was a "cowboy" feature. I grew up with Westerns and fell in love with them as he did. Our
1950's and 60's were filled with straight forward
television cowboys who were simple yet compli-
cated and told a complete tale in less than thirty
minutes.

The dime novel was the stuff Western glory was
made of and the *Lancer; Hero of the West* series is
my version of this 19th century genre. Part fact,
part fiction these books were always entertaining I
hope by reading my versions, your love for the
genre will grow as mine has over the years. In addition, the nice thing about these novels is they are
compact, can be read on short trip and read over
and over again.

I am excited for this series. So much so that as I
pen these words I am deeply involved in writing
Lancer's next adventure, *The Los Angeles Affair*. I
hope you will follow Lancer on my blog as well;
www.lancerheroofthewest.blogspot.com.

CHAPTER ONE

It was ten in the morning and Lancer was sitting by the window of his hotel room looking down on the bustling street below. The latest fashions from Paris must have just arrived. Mrs. Donaldson was admiring her new hat in the window of Johnson's Mercantile. More than one cowpoke glanced over their shoulder admiring the fine cut of a woman as she looked at their reflection in the glass. Joanie Donaldson never missed a chance to turn a gentleman's head. Even Lancer caught himself watching her strut.

The knock at the door disturbed him only for a moment but he didn't break stride in his coffee sipping.

"Who is it?"

"It is Javy, Senor Lancer," was the reply. "I have a telegram for you."

"Entra, mi amigo."

Javy Perez was as close to an employee as Lancer wanted. Aside from caring for his horse, he laid out his clothes and took his messages when they came in. In return Lancer paid him in gold for his services. A $20 gold piece here and there went quite a way, even in Tombstone. While things were getting more expensive in this silver boomtown, gold still held sway.

Perez handed the telegram to Lancer, who quickly opened it.

"Mr. Lancer. You will get a visit from my lawyer today. Mr. James B. Lovling ESQ. will fill you in on the details of why I want to hire you. He will pay your fee with a deposit up front which I believe will meet your requirements. Mrs. Sara Jane Paulson, Prescott, Arizona."

Lancer tossed a $20 coin to Perez.

"Javy, lay out my good suit," he said. "We are expecting some high class company."

Perez nodded and walked out of the room, heading toward the local tailor shop. Lancer had lost a few pounds lately and sent the suit out to be altered. It wouldn't do for one of Tombstone's most eligible bachelors to have his best suit looking just a bit shabby.

Lancer cast his eyes back to the street, but by now Mrs. Donaldson had become bored and moved on.

"She'll be back tomorrow," he mumbled with a smile.

It was time to head downstairs to see what the new day would bring. The creaky stairs at the Hotel Arizona needed work, but Lancer didn't mind. In his line of work it was good to get a warning from a creaky staircase in the middle of the night. It was like an alarm. More than once someone came a gunning for the famous Lancer and more than once those creaky stairs gave them away.

He could see the bright sunshine coming through the door as he headed to the bar to get a drink. Coffee followed by a shot of whiskey was his trademark morning pick-me-up. Bartender Jonah Rantz saw him coming and poured the drinks as he approached.

"Morning Mr. Lancer," Rantz said, greeting his predictable customer.

Lancer nodded and quickly downed the drinks, turning to survey the room as he did. Wyatt Earp was sitting at the Faro Table. Wyatt and his brothers Morgan and Virgil had arrived in town not long ago. Their reputation as lawmen preceded them, but Wyatt was having nothing of it. He said he had retired and with his woman, Mattie, had settled into the boomtown life. They were looking to strike it rich just like everyone else.

"Mr. Lancer," Wyatt smiled. "Have a go?'

Lancer sauntered over to the card table but Faro was not his game. He liked straight poker and a hand at craps when he needed the rush, but he was always pleasant to the former lawman.

"Not today, Wyatt. Say didn't your brother spend some time up in Prescott?"

Wyatt leaned back in his chair wondering what this freelance gunman had in mind and why he was inquiring about Virgil's past. Wyatt had only known Lancer for a short time but he knew his reputation. He was a gunman who specialized in helping folks find relatives, solving crimes and would do whatever they paid him to do as long as it was within the law. Lancer had ethics, which were difficult to find in anyone wearing a gun and no badge these days. Still Wyatt trusted few people in his life.

"Is there a reason behind the question regarding my brother's past whereabouts?"

Lancer nodded.

"Just some information about a local woman up there," he responded. "Perhaps a future employer."

Wyatt leaned forward in his chair again and called the gunman closer.

"Virgil was a lawman and a part-time politician in the mile high city. Had a go at lots of things and I'm sure he knew a lady or two. But I wouldn't spread that around if you know what I mean. He's happily married."

Lancer smiled.

"Where might I find him?"

Wyatt pulled out his pocket watch.

"Well, let's see. About this time he should be out of bed and eating breakfast," the former lawman grinned. "Down at the end of the street there is a small house with some roses out front. You'll probably find him on the front porch sipping coffee."

Lancer tipped his hat.

"Much obliged Wyatt."

Wyatt leaned back in his chair again before look-ing down at the game he loved so much. With a nimble set of fingers began shuffling the cards, ignoring the man whom he just chatted with.

CHAPTER TWO

Tombstone was a bustling town. Word had gotten out silver was rich in the region and folks were just starting to believe what they were hearing. It wasn't the gold rush of 1849, when massive numbers of wannabe rich folks headed for Sacramento, but it would do for a start. The speculators were still arriving and with them the whiskey drummers followed by the merchants. Since the town had an upper crust; there were high class ladies, a theater and Paris fashions. The fashions looked good despite the dirt which turned to mud every time heavy dew hit the streets.

Lancer walked the length of the street tipping his hat to the ladies as he did. The weather was dry but windy as usual. The sun shone down on an already hot morning. The women always smiled as Lancer walked by. He was good looking, stood tall in stature, and anyone who knew him liked him. All except a few gunslingers, because he plied his trade not only as a gentleman but as one of the good guys.

Lancer was known to greet children with a handshake. He greeted women with a smile and a nod. He didn't like crooks, charlatans or those who took advantage of people who were less fortunate than themselves. He came from good stock. Born in western Pennsylvania, the family name stood for old money. Lancer had some but no one knew how much. In fact, no one knew much at all about the man they called Lancer. They weren't even sure it was his real name. Some said he stole it after a near death experience. Some said it was taken from a medieval trade. Lancers were fighters on horseback who carried a lance to skewer their foes. One thing for sure; the man was educated. He'd often spout sayings from the classics or the Bard.

He joined the US Army at the age of 18, choosing the enlisted man's cause rather than a certain appointment to West Point. Lancer didn't particularly fit with the nose-in-the-air rich folks his family held with. Oh, he learned and practiced the finer things in life, including etiquette, but he'd rather spend his time with those he called "real people." Helping others seemed to give him a sense of purpose.

His fees were hefty, but there were times he charged what his clients could afford rather than leaving them in the cold wondering what might have been. His credit was impeccable and anyone who questioned his credibility or wallet hadn't been around Tombstone - or the West for that matter - very long.

Lancer came to the end of the street, and sure as Wyatt had said there sat Virgil on the porch, coffee cup in hand, taking in the morning sun. A small whiskey bottle sat nearby. The rocking chair looked inviting, positioned next to Virgil on the porch.

"Took you long enough to stop by and say howdy Lance," Virgil's gruff voice boomed from the front of the house.

"Well I guess I better say 'Howdy' back at you Mr. Earp!"

"Virgil, no formalities for a man who believes in the law, even out here. C'mon up and set a spell."

Lancer wandered up to the porch of the small home. As he did, Virgil got up and shook his hand, then turned to go into the house.

"The wife is off to pick a few berries for some pie tonight, so I'll have to get you a cup of coffee myself. Sugar?"

Lancer nodded and held up two fingers. Virgil disappeared into the house only to emerge a few moments later with a hot, steaming cup of black coffee.

"Mighty tasty. Mind if I put a shot of that red eye in?"

Virgil handed him the bottle and let his guest do the honors.

"Now to what do I owe the pleasure -or is this a social call?"

Lancer leaned forward and pulled the telegram from his boot and handed it to Virgil who raised an eyebrow when he read the few short sentences.

"And you want to know if I know these folks do ya?"

"It would be of some help to me, you knowing the social and community scene up in Prescott."

Virgil Earp, long and tall with a handle bar mustache he played with while thinking began to rock as he sat. He thought for a few moments, not knowing exactly how much information he should reveal to his new friend. A friend he only knew by reputation. The reputation must have been a good thing because Virgil decided to let loose with all he knew and it was plenty.

"Well to start off with, this lawyer, this Mr. Esquire…"

"Mr. Lovling," Lancer interrupted.

"There's nothing lovling about the man," Virgil shot back. "He's a snake in the grass and when he comes to town and you shake his hand, you check it right away. If you have all five fingers left I'd be shocked."

Lancer looked at his hands and wiggled his fingers. He then fingered his gun as if to say he'd shoot before he'd let the lawyer trick him in any manner. Virgil smiled and moved on.

The lawyer, Virgil went on to say, was well known in Northern Arizona and was the family barrister of Mrs. Paulson. He handled land grants and it was a major part of his business. He had gotten into some hot water with the acting governor, John C. Fremont, but he narrowly missed going to jail on fraud charges. He had some political connections that persuaded Governor Fremont to let him off with a warning. The newspapers seemed to play it up as a case of mistaken identity when it came to the fraud case. Virgil never believed the newspapers.

"Now as to the lady," Virgil continued. "I'm assuming she is the one you are the most interested in?"

In his own quiet way Lancer nodded again and smiled. He liked the ladies certainly and his respect for them was well known. He was also not easy to latch on to. He'd had romances but marriage was not his cup of tea. At least not anymore.

"Let me say this," Virgil continued. "She is a looker, you won't get any argument there from anyone. She's high class and I've never been able to figger if she was putting on airs. Sometimes I think she was, and then other times she was just as genuine as the new moon on a summer's night."

Lancer took it all in listening to Virgil wax eloquent about those he knew from his time in Prescott. Lancer figured he'd come to the right place.

"Husband?" Lancer asked.

"Oh yes, doesn't every pretty woman? Those that are not in the theater that is, have a husband somewhere along the way," Virgil smiled a sarcastic smile.

Lancer knew Virgil was making a reference to an actress who had come to town and who was pursuing Virgil's brother Wyatt. Josephine Marcus was in her own right a drop dead gorgeous woman, but one woman no man could place under thumb. Then there was Wyatt, who was the one man she couldn't bring under her spell. Virgil saw the gamesmanship in the pair.

"Would you liken Mrs. Paulson to Josie?" Lancer asked.

Virgil poured another shot of whiskey into his coffee and offered another to his friend. Lancer waved him off. The former Prescott lawman leaned back in his rocker and thought for a moment.

"Only in terms of outer beauty," he replied. "Josephine is head strong, knows what she wants and isn't afraid to go all out to get it, even if it puts her in an uncomfortable place."

"And Mrs. Paulson?"

"Won't do anything to embarrass herself, too much pride in her position in the community," Virgil sipped his coffee again. "Way too much pride."

Virgil shot up quickly in his chair as his wife Allie turned the corner from the sidewalk to the front porch walk. She was carrying a bag of groceries and a basket of berries. Virgil decided he should at least offer to carry them. As he got up he whispered to Lancer.

"Don't mention Josie around Allie," he said. "Hates her guts. And by the way if you are going to Prescott, Henry Paulson is a bit of a play around and he's loose with his wife's money. That's all I know."

Lancer nodded and started to get up with Virgil when Allie noticed him.

"Mr. Lancer, I do declare, I can't believe we haven't met yet," Allie said with cuteness in her voice. "Virgil been keeping you busy with some tall tales, has he?"

Lancer stood at the edge of the porch and, after Virgil took the groceries, the visitor held out his hand to the lady to usher her up the steps.

"No ma'am he's just been filling me in on life up north. Ya see I've taken a job up there, and, well, Virg here was kind enough to help me out with a little information on the town and its residents."

Allie brushed past him to the door, and then turned around to look him in the eye.

"No, Mr. Lancer, not its residents, more like its prominent citizens, I suspect," she said with a concerned tone in her voice.

Lancer put his head down and grinned.

"Well you got me there ma'am. I never was good at speaking around the truth when it came to a lady," he said in a shy manor.

Allie smiled back before entering the house. Virgil shrugged his shoulders as he looked at Lancer standing there. They both held back a laugh and settled for a smile and a handshake before Lancer headed back to the hotel where he'd wait for the attorney. He was grateful to Virgil Earp for the details and now thought he at least had something to go on.

He didn't know what the job was, but he already knew he was going to take it. The money was going to be assured - which wasn't his first thought in this particular case. The lady intrigued him. Mrs. Sarah Jane Paulson of Prescott, Arizona, was someone he looked forward to meeting.

CHAPTER THREE

Lancer sat quietly in the hotel lounge enjoying a drink away from the hustle of the gambling hall. Wyatt Earp continued to ply his trade as a Faro dealer and seemed to be having a good day, judging by the amount of folding money stacked up in his "bank." For Lancer's part, the *Daily Epitaph* was his concern this afternoon.

The newspaper filled him in on all the local news: who struck out, who struck it rich, who struck who with a bullet, and how many this month had died at the hands of one of the Cowboys. The Cowboys were a ruthless band of thugs who came over from Texas after the war. Actually they had been run out of Texas by the Rangers and then settled in Arizona. They were basically organized crime.

Curly Bill Brocius and Johnny Ringo were the best known among the Cowboys and led the gang on raids into Mexico quite often. When they weren't terrorizing local farmers and citizens the Cowboys were talking it up at the local saloons. Lancer didn't care for them, but so far they hadn't given him any reason to intercede. They were causing some concern for the Earp brothers, who had worked to clean up other towns from the likes of gangsters such as the Cowboys.

As he read his newspaper, Lancer heard a pair of horses ride up to the hotel Arizona. Looking through the glass window he could see trouble was right on his doorstep. It was Brocius and Ringo dismounting in quick fashion and heading through the door. The pair stopped dead in their tracks when they came face to face with Wyatt, who coolly ignored them while playing cards. Lancer knew there was a heavy duty handgun close to Wyatt's knee hidden under the table. Whether the Cowboy pair knew this, he wasn't so sure.

"Well if it ain't the famous Wyatt Earp, sittin' there dealin' cards, will you look at that?" Brocius turned to Ringo in making fun of the former lawman.

Wyatt just kept dealing cards although Lancer could see Wyatt adjusted his right leg to bring his knee - and the weapon - into a handier place. Lancer kept his distance, but his hand moved closer to his own weapon.

"What's a matter lawman, ain't no lawman left in you, you gotta play a dandy's game?" Brocius chided. "You ain't no law dog no more."

Wyatt just kept dealing, his head down and his hand ever closer to the handgun on his leg.

"Yeah, a dandy's game," Ringo jumped in.

Lancer could feel the tension begin to mount and decided to take action himself. He slowly sauntered over to the Faro table. He motioned to the three men playing to move on. They seized the opportunity to do exactly that, leaving their cash behind and moving into the lounge area. Lancer turned to Ringo and Curly Bill.

"I don't think I'd ever want to call Wyatt Earp a 'dandy' now gentlemen, especially when there is a Colt .44 pointing right at your guts with an itchy trigger finger, just aching to be scratched, holding onto it."

"You throwin' in with the Faro dealer are ya Lance?" Ringo said, half-challenging the gunman.

"Not that I need to. Y ou see I have the greatest confidence ole Wyatt here would drop the two of you before I even got my gun out of my holster," Lancer fingered his pistol. "So in that regard I'd have to say no, but just in case, you two know I just love to turn anything into a fair fight."

Ringo and Curly Bill stood their ground. Wyatt continued to turn over cards with his left hand. His right was firmly planted on the Colt, its hammer pulled back ready to fire. Ringo was anxious to try and knew he could always get off a good shot even if someone else got the drop on him. Wyatt knew it too, but he also knew the first rule of the West was not to give a faster gunman an even chance.

Time moved slowly as the four men grew even more anxious and their fingers moved closer to the handles of their guns. Suddenly a yell came from the street.

"Stage is a comin'!" An old man yelled.

The west bound stage was coming in hard and fast. The stage never came in that hard,and the old man squinted enough to inform the rest of the town there was something wrong.

"The driver is a'bleeding, he's been shot, look out, Injuns!"

The last words distracted the four men and while Wyatt and Lancer never moved their eyes away, Curly Bill and Ringo flinched. They turned to look at what all the yelling was about. As the stage pulled up right in front of the hotel, Bill and Ringo started for the door relaxing their hands away from their guns.

"You're off easy this time Mr. Lawman, but we'll be back," Ringo said sternly to Earp.

"I'm shaking in my boots, Ringo," Wyatt stared back.

Ringo and Bill moved on out the door and bumped into a tall, thin man with a mustache as they did. No apologies from the pair, but one came quickly from the incoming gentleman.

"Well, I do offer my apologies sirs, I guess I wasn't clear where I was going," the man said calmly and with confidence.

"Just watch where you're going dude," Bill said putting the man down. "Another dandy come to Tombstone. What is this place comin' to?"

Upon recognizing the gentleman, Wyatt jumped to his feet with a huge smile.

"Doc, Doc Holiday," Earp announced. "What in the hell are you doin' here?"

Wyatt rushed over and gave Holiday a big hug.

"Well Wyatt Earp I do declare," Holiday said. "I guess it was providence I should meet up with my old friend here in this gambling Mecca. How do you do?"

"I do just fine Doc, just fine, especially now you're here," Wyatt ushered his friend away from the table as Bill and Ringo stared at the pair before moving outside.

The two Cowboys stood in front of the hotel staring as the other men on the street tried as quickly and gently as possible to pull the driver down from the stage coach.

"Holiday, huh!" Bill grunted.

"He'll meet his too, don't worry about that," Ringo said with confidence. "This just hurries things along, my dream is nearly complete. Doc Holiday."

Bill stood in amazement at his confidence. Curly Bill wanted no part of Doc, who was known as one of the fastest in the territory. It was *that* lack of confidence versus the exuding confidence of Ringo that kept the pair together, or at odds, depending on the situation. Ringo considered himself the fastest and wasn't backing down from any fight with Holiday. In fact, he'd go out of his way to make sure they tangled.

Inside the hotel, Wyatt was busy introducing his old friend Doc to his new friend Lancer. Holiday made mention of the fact Lancer's reputation had preceded him, and, if it was any consolation to him, Holiday was a big fan and supporter of one Mr. Lancer. Both men had shady or at least interesting pasts which were kept secret by their own desire. Both came from money and both had left that money behind for reasons unclear to their friends and compatriots.

Wyatt asked Lancer to join them. Before Lancer could answer he noticed a man he thought might be Lovling, coming through the door.

"Thank you gentlemen but I think my appointment is here," Lancer said looking over at a large and portly man in a business suit.

"Oh, that one, I'd be careful of him," warned Doc. "I'm usually a pretty good judge of character and that character is not very good at all if I do say."

Lancer turned to Doc and shook his hand.

"Thank you sir, you are not the first person to warn me about the lawyer who acts like a snake oil salesman. Much obliged."

"Lawyer, well now I know I've avoided a snake bite," Doc replied with a sarcastic smile.

Doc nodded and along with Wyatt headed for the bar. Lancer straightened his clothes and headed for the lobby, where the large man was waiting and looking around somewhat lost.

"Mr. Lovling?"

"Yes, and you must be Mr. Lancer."

"Shall we have a drink in my room? I have a parlor as well."

"That would be most acceptable, sir. It's been a long, dusty and, if I do say, an exciting ride to your fair city," Lovling answered.

The two men walked up the winding staircase to Room 26 near the end of the hall. The pictures of Tombstone's finest graced the walls as they walked. Lovling could not help but sneak a glimpse as they moved along the hallway. He desperately wanted to ask Lancer about some of them, but his throat was parched. Stopping to talk would only delay the alcohol he was expecting to be served inside Lancer's room.

Lancer liked the end of the hall and kept the room as his own private home. Being near the last wall in the building gave him two things: an easy escape should he need one out the back door and down the steps; and second, easy access to an exit should a fire begin. Fires were not uncommon in Tombstone. With wooden buildings and a constantly blowing wind the chances for a quick spreading disaster were all too real.

The host pointed to an overstuffed chair as they entered the three room suite. Mr. Lovling quickly sat down. Lancer turned his back as he poured two drinks but Lancer would never do so unless he was facing a mirror. Lancer had strategically placed several mirrors on the walls in the suite so he could be more relaxed when holding court with company. He didn't trust Lovling, based on what Virgil Earp had given him.

Walking over to the parlor table, Lancer placed two drinks side by side, and Lovling quickly reached out for one of them. Watching him slap back the whiskey Lancer thought, this was a man who had had a long and nervous trip. He was reassured of this when Lovling placed the empty glass on the table in a manner as to say, "Another please!" His host obliged.

"So what are we talking about here Mr. Lovling Esquire?" Lancer asked as he lowered himself onto the sofa. "There was little to go on in Mrs. Paulson's message."

The lawyer pulled his leather valise to his lap and took out an envelope, handing it to the man in front of him. Lancer thumbed through it to find $1000 in cash and a bank check for $1000 more.

"I would have brought all cash but it didn't seem prudent, Mr. Lancer," Lovling pointed out. "And it is a good thing I did not after the trouble we ran into."

"Indians?"

"Thirty or 40 of those savages attacked us."

Lancer listened for a moment then motioned to his guest to move on with the reason for their meeting. Lovling paused for a moment to regain his thoughts and began again.

"First I should say Mrs. Paulson is a woman of some means so the payment is your retainer," the attorney said, moving to an official tone. "She will also cover your fee of $250 per day should your retainer run out before the job is done. She also insists in paying for a base amount of expenses, shall we say, $25 a day?"

Lancer nodded his approval and took another drink himself. He thought how well this new client had done their research for knowing all of his requirements in advance. Some information is on his card but not all the details. They must have contacted someone for information.

"So that is acceptable to you Mr. Lancer?"

"Yes, quite right depending on the job?"

The attorney again reached into his bag and pulled out a file. On top was a picture of a man.

"This is Mr. Paulson, Henry Paulson," Lovling said handing it to Lancer. "He disappeared about two weeks ago and hasn't been heard from since."

Lancer took the photo and took some time analyzing it.

"And you want me to find him?"

"Precisely," Lovling answered. "And any of the valuables he took with him."

Lancer raised an eyebrow. Now he was intrigued. Why on earth would the deserted wife, or maybe widowed wife, care about the valuables. Unless of course there was a dispute in the marriage and the jewels were caught in the middle.

"Valuables?"

"About $50,000 worth of jewels, cash, gold, all liquid for sure," Lovling responded.

"And you think he stole them?"

"We are not sure," the attorney answered putting the rest of his papers into his bag. "You will get further details when you get to Prescott. Right now I have a stage to catch. Do we have a deal?"

"When sorrows come, they come not as single spies, but in battalions," Lancer responded putting his glass down.

"Excuse me, sir?" Lovling queried.

"Shakespeare, Mr. Lovling, Shakespeare, and yes we have a deal," was the response. "What is your hurry? You aren't going to take part in our fair town's more enviable attributes?"

Lovling grabbed his bags, downed the last of the whiskey in his glass and headed for the door.

"No, Mr. Lancer I must be getting back."

The two men shook hands and Lovling opened the door to exit.

"Wait, here take this with you, it's a long ride to Prescott," Lancer tossed Lovling the rest of the bottle.

Lovling caught it and pointed it at Lancer.

"Much obliged," he said as he turned to leave. "You'll get more details when you get there."

As the door closed Lancer walked over to the window. From there he watched the stage being loaded and saw the oversized Mr. Lovling get in. Lovling kept a tight hold on the bottle however.

As the stage rode off on its way back north, Lancer walked around the room holding the photo of Henry Paulson. He was an interesting looking man and not any older perhaps than his wife, but the photo showed he was an intense man. Intense men don't abscond with the family jewels. Was he dead? Was he kidnapped? Is he a thief? He'd find out more when he got to Prescott.

"Javier! Pack my clothes for horse travel," Lancer shouted. "I'm leaving in the morning."

CHAPTER FOUR

It was 250 miles from Tombstone to Prescott across some of the most wasted land man ever set foot upon. However, once you reached the Yavapai Mountains and turned toward Prescott, the landscape changed from dusty and dry to the place where God rested on the seventh day. Up through the canyons and beyond Prescott to the mining town of Jerome and eventually to Flagstaff; these mountains were the most beautiful place on earth. They were also among the most dangerous. Due to its landing above sea level, Prescott was known as the Mile High City.

Lancer took his time and while he could have taken the stage, his trusty horse Lincoln, would never have made the rugged trip tied to a coach. Lancer was a northerner tried and true, and he distinguished himself during the recent War Between the States. At the first Battle of Bull Run, despite horrific losses by the Union, he urged his troops to stand strong. They did against overwhelming odds. For this he was boosted to the rank of Lieutenant with a battlefield commission. He was the youngest of his rank to that date.

Naming his horse Lincoln was not without its problems. He'd run into the occasional southerner along his way who despised the former President. Lancer's quick wit backed by his quick gun usually kept the conversation peaceful or at least moving along to a quiet conclusion.

The night sky was about to darken the landscape as the man in black decided to bed down for the night. It was chilly in the mountains but not as cold as it was a few short months earlier. A camp fire and some hot coffee might invite danger but there was no way he was running a cold camp. A clearing in a clump of trees would provide good cover, so he decided to call it a day.

As he gathered some firewood and dug a small pit, he thought about the local game. Deer would be nice, but wasting such a fine animal for one meal just wasn't his style. He didn't have the same feeling most women did about cute little bunnies so rabbit stew would fit his taste buds just right. He set up a small trap about 20 yards from camp, and it wasn't long before he heard the commotion of dinner running scared.

The small trap had caught a nice sized rabbit and he'd seen some wild turnips growing nearby. The few other vegetables he'd brought and a little salt pork would give him a fine feast. Skinning the rabbit would take a few minutes, but before Lancer did that he thought he should set some human traps of his own. There were Indians in the region and some were still hostile. More likely bandits would be the problem.

On long trips he always brought a few tiny bells like the kind you might string around the house during the holidays. The bells were just noisy enough to wake a man from a sound sleep if disturbed. He'd strung them to strings of rawhide with the purpose of encircling his camp with the bells tied to trees around him. If an intruder came in the middle of the night the bells would wake him.

As he skinned the rabbit he marveled at the giant trees around him and the peacefulness of silence. Only a brook nearby caught his ears. He couldn't help but think this was where God spent his final days creating the earth. It was as if he were listening to one of his uncle's sermons about the light and the dark and the seven days it took to create creation as it applied to earth. The green surrounded him with the white capped mountains far in the distance, but visible due to the supremely clean air. This was about as close to heaven as man was going to get he thought.

As he fried the rabbit and vegetables together he sensed a presence and set his gun, which lay on a rock to his side, into a more ready position. He turned it to a spot where he could very easily grab and fire if he needed to. The presence grew stronger but not a sound was coming from behind him.

"If you're hungry I have quite enough to share but I'd prefer you come out and identify yourself," Lancer said in a calm voice.

Behind him he could hear the brush moving as a man came forward.

"I would like that very much," the man said in a voice Lancer immediately determined was an educated Indian. "I also bring something to share with the man who kindly offers me his food."

Lancer turned to see a tall dark man dressed in deer skin clothing. He was clearly of the Yavapai tribe and looked very peaceful.

"Your English is spoken well," Lancer complimented the man.

"I have spent many years living amongst the white man," he countered. "I prefer to travel the mountains. May I sit?"

The host motioned to him to pull up a rock and have a seat. He pulled out a second metal plate and scooped some of the rabbit and vegetables into it and the Indian politely took it. He made fast work of the food, letting Lancer know his hunting lately was not as good as his host. He eyed the hot coffee and Lancer was more than ready as well, so he poured two cups.

"Lancer is my name," he said as he held out his hand to shake.

The hand was welcomed in return just as he'd learned from the white man.

"Charlie Green Dog," the Indian replied.

"Not your given name, I'm guessing?"

"No but most white men can't pronounce it and I'm not one to make trouble," he said. "It was the name given me at the mission school."

The two men got acquainted as the night rolled darker. The warm fire and the light it provided gave them reason to share a new-found friendship into the late hours. The visitor admired the fine horse, Lincoln. Lancer understood the Indian knew a good pony and thanked him for his admiration. Lancer informed him the government was talking about giving the Yavapai People their own reservation in the desert. Charlie Green Dog was not impressed. He had no intention of spending his remaining years on a reservation.

"I've seen enough of the white man's ways," he said. "I will not stand and fight. I will move on. There is plenty of country out there."

"For a wanderer?"

"For a wanderer," the Indian agreed. "Is that not wise, Mr. Lancer?"

"I do not think much of a man who is not wiser today than he was yesterday," Lancer replied as he looked to the multitude of stars layering the sky above.

"The saying of a wise man," Charlie Green Dog said showing respect to his generous host.

"A wise man indeed, so wise they killed him one night in a theater long before his time was due and before he finished the job he set out to do," Lancer said as he thought about the late president. "He was a great man indeed."

Charlie Green Dog looked over at the steed Lancer had tied to a tree.

"A man must be great if he chooses to name his horse and best friend after him," the Indian said, looking over at Lincoln. "That is the way to honor one you respect."

Lancer could only nod in agreement. He saw the Indian looking at the crossed lances on his holster.

He raised an eyebrow, caught easily by Charlie Green Dog.

"The symbols on your holster, tied to your name?" The red man asked.

"Crossed lances were a sign of medieval warriors, not unlike your people in times gone by," Lancer replied.

The Indian lowered his head, remembering the old days when his ancestors roamed the earth and the buffalo and elk were plenty. The days when a free man walked the earth and the only care he had was where to find his food for the new day. Lancer didn't need to speak of what his new friend was thinking. He'd seen it happen and knew what the greed of the white man had done. He still saw it today, which is why perhaps he chose the profession he did.

Lancer wanted a drink of whiskey but he knew to invite such a thing of an Indian was not only against the law but bad medicine. The night was going well so why spoil it?

Around ten o'clock the Indian startled Lancer when he changed the tone of the conversation

"Where are my manners, Mr. Lancer?" He asked. "I told you I had something for you, and your kindness to me must be shared."

Lancer had remembered his words from when they first met but lost it all in the conversation. What could this man offer him that was so special? He knew whatever it was he was obliged to take it. You don't snub someone like Charlie Green Dog. It would dishonor him and make things very bad.

Then the Indian pulled a small bottle out of his waist bag. He held it up to the light and inside was just enough to fill one finger of each coffee cup. Both were empty by now. He opened the bottle and threw away the cork, motioning to his host to push his cup forward. Lancer did as was expected.

"I think you call this Brandy," the guest pointed out.

Lancer looked at the drink in his cup and before drinking asked for the bottle. He studied it for a moment.

"Fine Napoleon Brandy my new-found friend," Lancer said with surprise. "And where might I ask did you get this?"

Charlie Green Dog looked to the sky and then around him before coming back and leaning into whisper to Lancer.

"A good Indian never tells, a drunken Indian might and since I can only be one of those, I will only say the man who carried this, carried it to his death, but someone else got the reward," Charlie Green Dog said pointing to the valley below. "They don't give rewards to Indians down there. My reward was a full bottle of this stuff and since I am an Indian who knows how to hold his liquor, I made the most of it."

Lancer accepted the explanation and held his cup to the sky to toast the man who brought it.

"A votre santé," Lancer said, saluting Charlie Green Dog in French.

"Merci," the Indian replied. "Never underestimate the value of an eastern woman coming west to teach in an Indian school. A Yavapai school no less."

The two men clinked cups and took a final nightcap. Lancer was impressed with the brandy.

"Damn fine brandy," he said. "And just the right nightcap."

The night was uneventful and he learned very quickly to trust the man who came into his camp and shared his food and a brandy with him. When the morning came Charlie Green Dog was gone. He'd left long before Lancer woke up but what he left was very impressive. The Indian had found a nest of large birds of which Lancer knew not. In the nest were two eggs large enough and just right enough to provide a morning meal.

Lancer surveyed the landscape but Charlie was nowhere to be found. He was grateful for the brief encounter with the peaceful soul who crossed his path. He was very grateful for the eggs which started his morning off right. Thinking back he could not think of a tastier brandy that he'd ever had. Maybe it was the moment itself, but it was a night he would not soon forget.

He was just three days out of Prescott when he came upon a wagon train full of future settlers. They were headed for the gold boom town of Wickenburg. Gold had been discovered after Henry Wickenburg settled there a dozen or so years earlier. It was still full of miners hoping to strike it rich but it was also the site where families were beginning to settle. The rugged mountains, the picturesque valleys, good water and abundant timber lent itself to all the makings of a community.

A church or two had sprung up amidst the filth gold mining brings. Lancer had seen it before. The gold, the gambling, the thieves, the criminals and the prostitutes. Hard earned money finding its way occasionally back home to the family but most of it left in the hands of a man who ran a card game and plied the miners with drinks. All the while a fancy lady stood by, hand on shoulder and at the right opportunity a hand in pocket. It was life in the boom towns.

"Mind if I ride along with you for a spell?" Lancer asked as he approached the wagon master.

Bill Royal was a decent looking man. Trusted, he shepherded his 10 wagons and the families they held, along the winding trails of the Wickenburg Mountains.

"Are you handy with a gun mister?" Royal replied spying the pearl handled pistol in Lancer's holster.

"As handy as I need to be," Lancer answered politely holding out his hand to shake. "Name's Lancer."

Royal shook and smiled.

"*The* Lancer?"

"The only one I know of. Why?"

"You remind me of a brash young Lieutenant I fought under at Bull Run," Royal said inquisitively. "Name wasn't Lancer though."

Lancer looked at him with a surprised smile. "You carry a union flag during the war?"

"I did, and I fought under an officer named Polk, Sam Polk, at Bull Run," as a smile came across the face of the wagon master. "Proud to say."

The two rode along for a few yards without saying anything until Lancer broke the silence.

"That was a tough day I hear."

Royal nodded knowing they both lost a lot of friends and colleagues at the first battle. They were confident young men going into the war. Mr. Lincoln had promised it would all be over in 90 days. Four years later the bloodiest war ever on American soil finally came to an end.

The wagon train was headed for Wickenburg. These settlers had banded together and purchased a huge lot of land in a nearby valley. They were going to set up a community. Among their number were a preacher, eight families with children, one with a baby on the way and a band of four unwed brothers who had come all the way from Italy. They brought grape vines along and were going to start a vineyard. They were a bit nervous around the campfire that night.

"Mr. Lancer, how do you know the area known as Wickyburg?" Geno asked in a thick Italian accent."

Lancer put down his plate of beans on a rock next to the fire and looked up at the stars. They shone bright that night, too many to count.

"You see those stars up there, my friend?" He asked of the young Italian, who nodded approvingly, while following Lancer's eyes to the sky. "I see this part of the country just like that."

Everyone at the edge of the fire listened intently to the man who seemed out of place in the west. He dressed well even when he wasn't in a suit. Wearing black leather chaps and vest, he was a fit man.

"Well you look at those stars and there are so many you can't count and I look at this land as the windmills turning in the breeze," he pointed out. "There are as many opportunities for a man out here as there are stars in the night sky. You just have to find the one that fits you and when you do you'll have your own piece of that wonderful sky above, right here on earth."

Royal walked up to Lancer with a bottle in his hand and offered Lancer a drink, which he gladly took. Dinner was coming to a close and some of the others got up to tend to their horses or bed the children down for the night. Lancer thanked Royal and headed toward his horse, which was tied on a string just north of camp.

As he walked a young lady followed him.

"Mr. Lancer," she raised her tiny voice a bit stopping the man whom she summoned. "Mr. Lancer, may I speak with you?"

Lancer turned to the lady with a smile. Her blond hair up in a bun revealing her very attractive face above her just as attractive figure. Her long neck seemed inviting as Lancer tried not to be enticed by this rare beauty. She was a handsome woman he had noticed at dinner but he didn't say anything assuming she was probably married and he wasn't ready for a confrontation. She walked alongside Lancer as they moved across the camp.

"You are a bit of a philosopher, Mr. Lancer, something I did not expect from a man with your reputation," she queried.

"And what reputation is that Miss…"

"Hanna, Hanna Burns."

"Miss Hanna Burns?"

"Well the reputation of a gunslinger," she smiled at Lancer. "It is rare that a man who carries a gun as his profession should philosophize about the stars as if he were Don Quixote."

Lancer stopped in his tracks and faced the woman directly. A stern look replaced his smile.

"There will be windmills here as well, Miss Burns, but those windmills will be put up by you and they will bring water to the surface to cool the land and to water what I hope will be grapes made into the finest Chianti money can buy," Lancer pointed out in a strong tone. "People who live in the West, Miss Burns, are not uneducated about the finer things in life. It's just if they've never lived anywhere else, it takes them a little bit to grasp the concept of something other than food on the table, clothes on their back and a fire in the fireplace to keep them warm."

Hanna put her head down realizing she had been put in her place by an educated man who also carried a gun. Lancer was feeling good but not all that good as he fell just short of a tirade. The woman's beauty kept his temper in check.

"I do apologize Mr. Lancer," she said shyly. "I guess I really did speak out of turn."

"It's Lancer, just Lancer," he said smiling as he turned away to attend to his horse, leaving Hanna standing all alone.

Hanna watched him go, realizing this really was a remarkable man and he'd be a good catch some day. As he disappeared into the darkness she looked at the stars above. She smiled and headed back to her wagon where her brother was tending to the cooking utensils. Hanna Burns, a very headstrong woman, had met her match.

CHAPTER FIVE

The tall timber surrounding Prescott gave the land lushness only an admirer of such natural beauty could handle. Prescott was set in a wide valley in the heart of the mountains and as Lancer reached the summit he looked down on the growing city as it sat one mile above sea level. The nickname of "The Mile High City" was appropriate.

Atop Lincoln, Lancer sauntered into town and noticed the sign proclaiming the real dichotomy of this western village-gone-wild.

"Prescott. We have more bars than churches!"

The proclamation wasn't too far from wrong. Indeed, there were a lot of bars in Prescott, but there were just as many churches. It seemed the bars held more people during the day and on at least six nights during the week. Sunday most of the bars closed so the townsfolk could atone for their sins. Sunday, all the churches were filled.

From its heyday Prescott was centered on a large town square. In the middle was the courthouse, while on every avenue around the courthouse sat a bar, or two or maybe even three. The churches were on the outskirts of town just beyond the boarding houses. Lancer headed for the newspaper office just down the road a piece.

The Prescott Courier was a well-known newspaper with very few political sides being taken, although it did publish an editorial page. Not like the *Tombstone Epitaph* which took a certain political stance and stuck with it. The *Courier* was well run and a fair journal. Lancer felt it was a place to start to get a little recent background on the case he was about to embark upon.

The *Courier* office wasn't too far out of the mainstream of town, just on the fringe of what could be called downtown Prescott. Lancer rode up, hitched Lincoln to the bar out front and walked on in even before stopping for a drink.

A young man sat right up front with a pencil and pad. Jonah Wiles did double duty. He was the paper's main reporter but he also served as a receptionist and emptied the trash when it came time. Such was the life of a journalist in a town growing out of its roots exponentially.

"May I help you sir?"

"Just looking for a little information," Lancer answered. "Do you have some back copies of the paper I can read? I want to do a little research."

Wiles got up and pulled out the last four weeks of issues which totaled 12 pages of the newspaper. Far from a daily newspaper The *Courier* only printed three times a week and usually only ran one page on both sides. Until recently the news was pretty dry as Lancer noticed right on the front page was the name of his client.

"Henry Paulson Gone Missing" the headline stated only a short time back.

"Thank you, this will do just right," Lancer said as he placed the folded newspapers under his arm and walked out. He and Lincoln rode off to find a place to call home for a few weeks.

Unbeknownst to Lancer, across the street sat Lawyer Lovling in a diner. His eyes popped out when he saw Lancer exit the newspaper office. He thought his office would be the first place the hired gun would visit and not the local newspaper. Lovling thought to himself this was a very thorough and well-thought-out man he'd hired. He quickly finished his lunch and walked out. He had to see his client now.

The Paulson home was on the West end of Prescott, where all of the more well-heeled people lived. The street was right out of the East, matching Philadelphia, Boston and even Atlanta for its elegance and opulence. These were wealthy people, and they wanted everyone to know it. A carriage arrived in front of 33 Buttermilk Lane. Mr. Lovling exited the carriage and made the trek up the walk to the front door of the large yellow trimmed home.

A knock on the door brought a thin black woman dressed in a black dress with a white apron. She smiled upon seeing Lovling and ushered him into the front room.

"Wait right here Mr. Lovling, I'll git Miss Sarah for you, she's just upstairs," the maid said.

Lovling nodded and sat down on the expensive sofa which obviously came from someplace in Europe. Germany perhaps, possibly, Austria. The Eagles engraved into the wooden arms gave some credence to Austria. It wasn't long before Lovling heard someone coming down the stairs. Sarah Jane Paulson entered the room.

She was tall and statuesque. Sara Jane had been to the best schools in the East until her family moved to Prescott when she was a young debutante about to come out. Her father had made his fortune in banking and lost much of it dabbling in railroads. He regained enough of it in the cattle business to set up his wife and daughter with a substantial amount before his untimely death. She was not quite a millionaire but she had money. Her mother, getting on in years, lived in the house as well. A feisty woman, she never put on the airs her daughter and son-in-law did. Mother didn't come from money. She made it the old fashioned way: she let her husband earn it and she spent it.

"He is here, he arrived in Prescott just today," Lovling said as he got up from the sofa. "He stopped at the newspaper office first, probably to get more information. I think he's very good, perhaps too good."

Sarah Jane walked over to the other sofa and sat down. A tray was already on the table with several glasses and a pitcher of chilled lemonade. Elmira, the maid, had done her job superbly. She'd taken care of the drinks and a small plate of tea cakes sat beside it. Now she was nowhere to be found unless summoned.

"I wanted to hire the best, Mr. Lovling," Sarah Jane said in an understated tone as she poured two glasses of the cool drink. "It wouldn't do to have this done as a shabby effort now would it?"

"No it would not," answered Lovling. "It's your call but we need to stay on our toes."

She leaned back and took a pleasant drink, lifting a tea cake off the plate as she did.

"If something takes him off the track we'll bring him back on track," she said coyly. "You know his reputation with the ladies, and, well, least of all I am a lady."

Lovling placed a tea cake in his mouth and grinned before washing it down with the lemonade. He knew all too well the persuasive nature of Sarah Jane Paulson. She was smart, she was cunning, and she was beautiful. This was a tough combination to beat, especially in a woman with such wealth.

"What's going on in here?" The voice of Miley Miller shattered the air as she entered from the kitchen. "Oh, it's you, Loving?"

"That's Lov-ling, mother, Mr. Lov-ling," Sara corrected her mother's mispronunciation.

"Loving, Lovling, who the hell cares?" Miley fired back as she reached for a glass of lemonade. "You got anything stronger than this lemon wiz, missy? I'm sure Mr. Lovesick here would like a drink too, right?"

Lovling looked at Sarah Jane with an inquisitive smile, not knowing what to say until she nodded her approval.

"Why yes, Mother Miller, I'd like that," the lawyer offered up. "Gin perhaps."

The old woman fumed back at him.

"I ain't your mother and don't you ever address me that way, you old bag of wind," Miley fired back. "You got that mister?"

"Why yes, Miley, I do," he said squeamishly.

"And don't ever address me common either. It's Mrs. Miller to you!"

Lovling put his glass down nervously and backed off not knowing how to address the old woman who'd just emasculated him verbally. Sarah Jane ignored them both until Miley spoke up again. This time she brought up Henry.

"So have you found out anything about that good-for-nothin' son-in-law of mine yet, Mr. Lawyer?" Miley raised her voice then lowered it as Elmira entered the room with a tray and a bottle of gin along, with two glasses. "Thank you Elmira. Just set it on the table and we'll pour it ourselves."

"Yes'um," she answered as she walked out.

Lovling sat stunned again. He wasn't used to such abruptness from someone he couldn't fire back at. The old woman was challenging him in every way possible and he was on his heels. He tried to muster something – anything - and decided to pour them both a drink. As he sipped on his, Miley threw hers back and pushed again.

"Well, have you? Found out anything?"

"No but we're following some leads," he answered.

"We've hired an investigator, mother," Sarah Jane finally spoke up. "A man-for-hire out of Tombstone."

"Tombstone!" Miley shouted. "There ain't nothin' but liars and cheats in Tombstone. Where is he?"

Lovling went on to describe how Lancer had just arrived in town and he expected a visit any hour now. He would probably go straight to the law office but then again he might show up on the Paulson's door step. He was unpredictable but the best and Henry deserved the best.

"Henry is a no good liar and a cheat and I'll never understand why you married him," Miley said, looking directly at Sarah Jane. "Never."

"We were in love mother, and we were young," she answered.

"Young, yes," Miley responded. "Love? No. Lust? Yes, but love? No. I should have tied your legs together when you were 16."

"Mother!" Sarah Jane yelled. "We have company."

"He's not company, he's your lawyer and a real snake in the grass if I do say so," Miley said, indignantly before stomping off.

Sarah Jane began to weep and Lovling moved over to comfort her. She recomposed herself quickly, not allowing him the pleasure of putting his arm around her and making a move. She'd seen him work before. He loved money more than anything and making a move on a grieving woman was just his style. She wiped her tears and got up to show him the door.

"I'll be in touch," she said as she ushered him out and closed the door.

CHAPTER SIX

The Palace Saloon on Montezuma Street was
barely open a couple of years but was wide open
for business every day of the week. It was even
open on Sunday. The owners didn't cotton with
the attempt by local churches to shut down its
business, so consequently Sunday was usually the
best day of the week for the owners of the Palace.

Lancer tied Lincoln to the post out front and
walked inside. Gas lamps were the new thing in
the East and sure enough, Lancer thought to himself, it would be right proper for the Palace to
sport its own. They were the first things Lancer
spotted as he entered the music-filled cabaret.
Tombstone had some of the best saloons in the
West, but the Palace would outshine anything
down South.

Above the bar stood a sign proclaiming "The best
rooms west of the Mississippi." An arrow pointed
around the corner to the registration desk. Lancer
passed on a drink and headed to the check-in desk
where he found a burly man with a bow tie. He
thought the tie looked out of place on this portly
gentleman with the beard, but who was he to
judge.

"Need a room, preferably one at the end of the hall
if you have it," Lancer told the man.

Barry Grister paused for a moment, never lifting
his head.

"An unusual request to say the least, mister," Grister replied. "New cowboys in town usually want to

be closer to the other end of the hotel, you know, where the ladies are more readily available."

"Nope, the end of the hall is just fine for me," Lancer reiterated. "I need my sleep and I find it's a little quieter down there, if you catch my drift."

Grister never looked up but laughed out loud with his head down.

"You got me there pardner," he replied. "How's about number 15 down at the north end? That will be $10 in advance per night or $50 for the week."

Five $20 gold pieces fell quickly onto the table in front of Grister, who stopped in his tracks, paused and slowly looked up.

"Who are you mister?"

"Just a man who is going to be around for a couple weeks," Lancer said, as he reached for the register to sign it. "Are you a man who can provide information when needed?"

Grister looked down again preferring not to make eye contact with Lancer. Another $20 gold eagle fell onto the table. The proprietor took the coin and placed it in his shirt pocket.

"What do you need to know?"

"Call that an advance. I'll let you know when I need an answer."

Lancer picked up his gear and the key and headed up the stairs to his room. Grister watched the new guest closely. Lancer found his way to the end of the hall, checked the back door to find out it was locked, and then turned to enter his own room.

The room was just as the sign said. It was spacious, had finer linens, a water filled jug on the table and even a bathtub in the corner. It had all the comforts of home except there was only one room instead of three. There was even a complementary bottle of whiskey on the dresser.

"This is alright," Lancer spoke out loud before opening the bottle and taking a swig. "Yup this is alright."

He tossed the newspapers and his basic gear on the dresser. He figured it was time to get some dinner and find someone to bed down his horse for the night. Keeping his gun belt in place Lancer walked down to the bar where he ordered a shot of whiskey and some information. He wanted a nice big steak. The bartender pointed out the Palace was also a restaurant and some of the finest steaks in the territory were cooked right there.

The shot of whiskey went up to his mouth but before he could drink it, a cowboy bumped into him while dancing. Consequently, the drink went all over the bar, just missing Lancer's shirt.

"Will you look where you're going, mister?" Lancer suggested with a strong tone in his voice.

"Stay out of my way dandy, I'm dancing on the dance floor," came the man's reply.

The talk got the best of Lancer and he reached over and tapped the man on the shoulder.

"I'd like an apology mister and 'stay out of my way dandy' isn't going to do it," Lancer demanded.

The man stopped dancing and pushed his partner out of the way. The music stopped as the crowd began to encircle the pair. Trouble was a'brewin'.

"Well maybe you should stay out of my way, dandy before I make little mince pies out of you."

Lancer watched the man's right hand as it moved closer up on his hip ready to draw if need be. He didn't want any trouble but it looked as if the cowpoke did. As the man went for his gun Lancer quickly grabbed his upper right arm, spun him to the right, and with his own right arm locked the man's gun arm behind his back. The cowboy's gun went off as he tried in vain to grab it. The bullet grazed his own right thigh sending blood spattering.

Lancer drew his own gun out of his holster and with the barrel struck the gunman on the back of the head rendering him unconscious. The cowboy fell quickly to the floor as the woman he was with rushed to his side. He was out cold but certainly alive. His leg was still bleeding.

"Call this man a doctor, somebody, quick!" Lancer raised his voice.

The dance hall girl looked up at Lancer angrily.

"You didn't have to shoot him!"

The crowd laughed at the remark, for Lancer did not shoot him. He shot himself.

"Hey lady, you're backing the wrong pony in this race," said Grister. "Tommy there shot his own leg and this guy probably saved Tommy's life."

A commotion at the front of the saloon began as Sheriff Hank Jackson entered with his gun drawn and shotgun in the other hand. A deputy walked behind him.

"What's going on here?" Sheriff Jackson proclaimed.

"It was self-defense sheriff," said one bystander. "This fella here got the drop on Tommy when Tommy tried to pull his gun."

"That so?" The sheriff asked of Lancer who nodded the affirmative. "Is he dead?"

"No just a bit embarrassed," the girl said dropping her head. "He shot himself in the leg trying to get the gun out of his holster."

The sheriff began to laugh and the rest of the customers joined in. Lancer did not. He knew the seriousness of what happened.

"Tommy never could shoot straight," Sheriff Jackson added. "Who are you mister? Let me buy you a drink."

The two men turned to the bar and the sheriff put two fingers in the air to the bartender who responded immediately. He poured two strong drinks. The two men clinked their glasses together before downing the hard liquor. Jackson pointed to the glasses again and the bartender refilled them.

"You must be pretty good to get the drop on ole Tommy," Sheriff Jackson said holding out his hand. "I'm Hank Jackson and you are?"

"Lancer, outta Tombstone."

"Ah yes Mr. Lancer, I've been expecting you since the disappearance of Henry Paulson. I've got some ideas. Maybe we can discuss them over coffee at the jail tomorrow."

A thank you was in order and Lancer nodded in the affirmative. It was not always the case where the local lawman wanted Lancer's help. Most wanted him out of the way until the case was solved and then they sent him packing. All guts and no glory but maybe not this time. Sheriff Jackson seemed like a decent sort.

"Thank you sheriff, I'd like that but why don't you join me here for coffee say about eight o'clock?"

"Sounds like an offer I can't refuse, Mr. Lancer, see you then."

The sheriff departed. Lancer finished his drink and turned to the bartender.

"Where do I bed down my horse for the night?"

The bartender pointed over his shoulder, noting there was a large gap between the buildings. It was large enough for a man and a horse.

"Livery is two blocks down that way."

Lancer thanked him kindly and walked out.

"Much obliged."

He unhitched Lincoln so he could take the horse down the side street and to the stable for the night. As they walked down the dark alley Lancer felt confident. He was still in control and could still handle himself despite the fact every young punk in the West, it seemed, had an axe to grind.

All of a sudden the uncomfortable feeling of round cold steel laid against his back made him stop dead in his tracks. Lancer raised his arms instinctively. One of his hands held the reigns of the powerful horse Lincoln. Lancer didn't have time to realize this might be the last time he knew the horse as a companion. He didn't say a word preferring to let the man with the gun make the first move. He had gotten the drop on Lancer and the man from Tombstone had no idea why.

Was it a robbery? Was it a friend of Tommy's maybe seeking a reckoning? Either way, he wondered, how on earth could he let someone get the drop on him so easily? Then suddenly his mind was shattered.

"Don't move mister, I'm a crack shot," came the voice of a young woman. "Don't turn around and just walk real slow down this here alley to the livery."

"A woman?" Lancer questioned. "A woman got the drop on me?"

The young lady didn't say a word but kept the barrel of her gun pressed against his back. Lincoln followed along as they walked.

"Who are you and what do you want?" Lancer questioned again.

"Just shut up and keep walking."

He did as he was told, eyes roving, looking for an opportunity when none was there. Finally the pair reached the livery stable. The streets were only lit in this part of town when the moon traversed from behind the clouds. The woman made sure when she crossed the street to the barn where the horses stood for the night, the full moon was hidden by those clouds.

As they approached, Lancer opened the door with his hostage taker right behind. It was here he seized his opportunity. She followed close behind but as she did she momentarily let her guard down as Lancer walked through the door. He grasped this in an instant and slammed the door shut on her arm. Fortunately her weapon did not go off but it fell to the floor.

The freed man-for-hire quickly tackled her and threw her to the ground. He landed on top of her. His strength was overpowering and she was subdued.

"Now if you promise to behave yourself and tell me what this is all about I'll let you get up with your dignity still intact," Lancer pointed out with a half-smile. "If not I'll just have to call the sheriff or turn you over my knee myself and I can assure you there will be no dignity in that."

"Okay, let me up."

"Not until you tell me your name."

"Willie, Willie Miller."

Lancer pondered for a moment as he knew this was a soft young girl but with a man's name. It was the same name as the family of the missing man whom he was hired to find. He was confused.

"Willie, your name is Willie?"

"It's short for Wilamena, now can I get up or are you going to rape me right here on the ground?"

He got off the woman and picked up her fallen handgun before she could reach it.

"I wasn't going to rape you, little missy," he said. "And you better think twice before pulling a gun on a man in a dark alley. Now what's this all about?"

"Can I have my gun?"

"Not until I get some assurance you aren't going to shoot me."

Willie went on to tell Lancer she was the niece of Sarah Jane and Henry Paulson. The daughter of Sarah Jane's late brother, Billy Joe Miller. He disappeared a year ago. Everyone thought he was dead but a body was never found. They finally got a letter from him, which came from Philadelphia saying he ran out and wasn't coming back.

"I knew my father better than that," Willie pointed out. "He'd never do that, run out on us."

"Go on," Lancer urged.

She continued to tell him how she and her mother lived in a modest house just outside of town a ways. Willie said she didn't trust her Aunt Sarah. Not that she liked her Uncle Henry much, but she just didn't trust her Aunt.

"So why pull a gun on me?"

"I was confused," she said, bowing her head. "You are working for her and I'm sure they are using you to prove Uncle Henry ran off and abandoned her like they say my father did. You are on their side."

He took the gun and handed it back to Willie, then took Lincoln to a stall to bed him down.

"I'm not on anyone's side Willie, I'm just a man hired to do a job," he said taking the saddle off his horse.

"You're getting paid by her."

"I get my pay no matter what the outcome, but if the answers lead me to a crime I take the criminal to the authorities," Lancer said heading back to the young lady. "I'm not a criminal and I don't throw in with criminals. And I don't like having the barrel of a .44 stuck in my back."

"Billy Loest told me I might have trouble with you."

Lancer looked at her with an inquisitive eye.

"The bartender," she fessed up.

"The man who sent me down a dark alley to the livery stable?"

"Billy Loest," she repeated. "He was my father's best friend."

Lancer took her by the arm and began ushering her out the door when he stopped and realized he hadn't paid the livery man for Lincoln's keep. He looked around for a moment when Willie held out her hand.

"Six bits," she said. "I work here part time."

Lancer could only laugh as he pulled two dollars out of his vest pocket and handed it to Willie.

"Keep the change, you earned it."

The pair giggled as they walked back down the street. They stopped in front of the Palace but remained out of sight of the patrons.

"You'll keep in mind what I said?" Willie asked.

"I will, but only if you promise to keep your gun holstered when my back is turned," he said with a smile.

She grinned, lowering her head. He kissed her on the forehead, realizing someday this was going to be a beautiful woman but for now she was simply a 15-year-old girl who had lived a lot of life.

"Now go on home and I'll let you know if I need your help."

All of a sudden her smile turned into a shy grin. It was the kind of grin a daughter gives to a loving father. In her eyes Lancer had turned from a man she might have killed to the father she lost not long ago. She did as he said and skipped home. Lancer watched her go. He was going to return to the Palace very quickly.

Upon entering the front door he looked toward the bar. His steely eyes met the shocked look of bartender Billy Loest. Neither man said a word. Their eyes told more than any conversation could. Then suddenly Lancer smiled a huge grin, ordered a steak sent to his room and headed up the stairs. Billy Loest was lost for any kind of words.

CHAPTER SEVEN

Lancer didn't sleep well his first night in Prescott.
Maybe it was the room, the bed or the case he was
embarking on which he wasn't sure about. It certainly wasn't the noise from the Palace Dance
Hall. He'd heard louder and worse in Tombstone.

Before going down to breakfast he checked his
handgun, making sure it was clean and ready to
use if needed. He also checked his derringer which
he kept in his vest pocket. The dual bullet Zig Zag
was a leftover from his earlier days but it never
failed him when he needed it. Most tiny handguns
held one shot and were only accurate at close
range. Usually when needed to stop an aggressor
they failed. Lancer liked the dual shot ZZ because
if the first one didn't do the trick chances are he
would be close enough to the intended to put a
second bullet in a more deadly part of his oppo-
nent's body. He also kept a small handgun just in
case. Times were unpredictable in the West.

The life of a gun-for- hire held its own challeng-
es. Sometimes the case you take was helping
someone who needed it. Often it was just the opposite. Lancer previously ran the question through
his mind, "Why on earth did I get involved in this
one?" As he went down to breakfast these
thoughts were paramount on his mind. Maybe bacon and eggs with a side steak would make the
day and the case go somewhat better.

Sheriff Jackson was already in the dining room
sipping on a cup of coffee when he spied Lancer

heading toward him. Jackson stood up to shake and Lancer obliged.

"I took the liberty of ordering coffee and I'd recommend the steak and eggs," Jackson said as the waiter approached.

"Sounds good sheriff," Lancer replied turning to the waiter who stood by. "Medium with three eggs over easy and a side of buttermilk biscuits."

"I'll have the same," Sheriff Jackson added.

The two men sat quietly for a moment before Jackson stepped up.

"So what do you know so far, Mr. Lancer? About the Paulson's I mean?"

"Well, not a lot, but I'd be pleased if you would fill me in some."

Sheriff Jackson wasn't a country bumpkin but he wasn't a legal scholar either. He knew he'd have to give to get and started right in telling what he knew to date. He discussed how Henry Paulson was a businessman who fancied himself a bit wiser than he actually was. Paulson did well but a bad turn of a card, an investment which didn't pan out and then he had to borrow the money. Jackson knew Paulson's credit was at a limit with the banks so he had queried around about other means of loans.

"What about his wife? She's well off I understand."

Sheriff Jackson rubbed his chin before offering. Paulson has pretty much been cut off by Sarah Jane. Except for necessities Henry was on his own, so he had to seek out other means.

"Other means?" Lancer asked. "I'm afraid you have me at a loss."

"He sought out some of the less upstanding folks in town who had money and hadn't made that money by the most legal of ways."

Lancer nodded.

"Ken Golder is one such person," Jackson brought up. "Mr. Golder owns a large spread east of town, runs 1500 head of cattle normally and sometimes the herd swells as some of the other ranchers herds diminish if you catch my drift?"

"I do," Lancer replied.

"In fact, it was one of Golder's men who met with Paulson right before he disappeared."

"You have a name?"

"Mitchell Gatt, hired gun and he's also disappeared."

The steaks arrived and the two men continued their conversation over the meal. At first bite Lancer realized everyone was right about one thing: The Palace did have the best steaks around. More coffee was poured before the sheriff offered up more interesting news.

"And there was a woman too," he blurted out. "Jenny Francis is a dance-hall girl at the Prescott Town Hall Hotel. She and Paulson had gotten mighty close and I am sure Sarah Jane knew about it."

This was powerful information for Lancer. He and the sheriff continued to talk through breakfast and capped it off with a shot of rye before Lancer departed. The sheriff pulled out his wallet but Lancer would have none of it. He dropped the cash on the table and thanked Jackson for his help. Jackson smiled as he got up and walked out ahead of Lancer heading back to his office.

The Palace was known for its steaks, and a five ounce steak with a side of bacon and three eggs were all the man in black needed. Well, that and two cups of strong coffee with a bit of sugar. There was no denying Lancer's sweet tooth. As a child growing up his mother knew he had a penchant for two unusual tastes in sweets. First there was French chocolate. Second was a rare taste for anyone except a family with money: Turkish Delight.

Even today, Lancer had a weakness for the latter but rarely found it. Until now. As he walked toward the door, something caught his eye. The Palace had a confectionary counter with a sign proclaiming "Straight from the Exotic Parts of the World." He couldn't help but wander over and there to his surprise under the glass case sat a stack of boxes marked "Turkish Delight."

"Can I help you mister?" The voice of the Mexican clerk broke Lancer's dreaming.

"You don't see that much around anywhere?" Lancer said pointing to the candy.

"All the way from Istanbul."

"Most people don't even know where that is my friend."

The Mexican thought for a moment before answering.

"I don't know where that is, senor," he came back. "All I know is it tastes really nice."

Lancer smiled before putting up two fingers indicating he wanted two boxes. The clerk was taken aback because he knew even a piece was more than most cowpokes could afford and this man was ordering 20 pieces. His mind was put at ease as Lancer pulled out two $20 gold pieces and plopped them down on the counter.

"I'll wrap them for you?"

"No, just deliver one to my room here at the hotel and I'll take the other with me," Lancer replied.

The clerk did as he was told and Lancer walked out with the box in hand.

The ride to the Paulson home was an easy one. Prescott, despite some of its dirt roads and bars, was a pretty sophisticated place. The rich, who didn't live here but lived down in the warmer climates, would have a summer home to visit when it got too hot in the desert. Lancer rode tall in the saddle but kept his eyes open for anything out of the ordinary. It was his way. He'd always been good at spotting things which would mean more to him later. To say he was someone who paid close attention to detail was an understatement. It was probably something the woman on the wagon train would be surprised to learn, given the fact in his profession he also carried a gun. The thought brought a smile to his face.

The big house came into view just a few doors down but the rider chose to pass on by. He wanted to scope out the neighborhood first, see what he was letting himself in for. As he rode by, he saw Elmira on the front porch. She noticed him as well, but he kept on riding. Lancer hoped she didn't get a good glimpse of him because he didn't want anyone to know how he worked. Lincoln continued on down the path.

Elmira walked through the door and moved right to the window. She pulled back the curtain and watched the rider until he was out of sight.

"Anything wrong Elmira?" Came the voice of Sarah Jane from the bottom of the steps behind her.

"Oh, nothing ma'am," she answered. "Just looking out to make sure I didn't miss anything while sweeping the porch."

"Well get on with your work inside please," she said. "I'm expecting a male visitor today."

"Yes 'um, right away," Elmira said, scurrying away from the window and toward the kitchen.

As Lincoln came to the end of the street Lancer noticed an alley way to his right which obviously ran behind the row of homes. He chose to take a ride down the alley to see the Paulson home from the rear. At the back of the property stood a small barn, more like a livery actually. Inside obviously was a carriage used by the Paulson family for special occasions or maybe just going to town. A buckboard stood near but outside.

A board was out of place not far from the gate.

"Whoa," Lancer pulled back on Lincoln's reins and dismounted to take a closer look.

What he saw was what he was hoping for. There was a spot of blood and some fiber, perhaps from a shirt or pants. It had not been there long and while not fresh, it was probably only a couple of weeks old. Lancer pulled out his knife and carved out the place where the spot of blood blended into the wood. He put it into his saddlebag and moved on.

Arriving at the front of the home Lancer looked up and down the porch. He didn't even have the time to knock before Elmira opened the door. Lancer was surprised when the maid greeted him with less than a smile.

"Mr. Lancer would you like to come in?"

"Well that depends. Is Mrs. Paulson at home?"

"You know she is Mr. Lancer," was her smile-less reply. "You've been checking out the comings and goings for the better part of an hour."

"Was it that obvious?"

Elmira didn't say a word but opened the door even wider to usher the man in. He smiled easily as he entered. Elmira pointed to the sofa and Lancer did as he was shown. The maid disappeared to summon the lady of the house. It wasn't long before the tall, lean, good looking woman arrived. She was dressed finer than the lady of the house should during the middle of the day.

As he stood up Lancer tried not to be obvious in his admiration of the woman, hoping to make a more professional impression than one of man to woman. It was difficult because Sarah Jane was a knockout and her beautifully lined body held sway even before you saw her face. He was impressed, impressed enough to take her hand and kiss it as he greeted her.

"Well, I'm impressed with your manners, Mr. Lancer, I've heard of your prowess with the ladies," Sarah Jane said with a bit of a blush.

"Beauty such as yours should be held on high Mrs. Paulson, such beauty is a gift from God and all I can do is to admire the Master's handiwork," was his reply as he lifted his eyes and escorted her into the living room where they sat opposite each other.

"Coffee Mr. Lancer?"

"Lancer, please, and yes I'd love some."

"Elmira," she raised her voice before turning to see the family maid already a few feet away.

"Coffee, yes'um right away ma'am," she responded. "Cream and sugar, Mr. Lancer?"

Lancer held up two fingers to indicate the sweetness. The nod of approval was all Elmira needed and she was gone. She was quick to return with a silver tray full of coffee, the fixin's and some orange flavored sweet cakes. She handed Lancer a napkin and placed a couple of the cakes on a plate along with a fork. He took them with a smile.

"Elmira is famous in these parts for her orange sweet cakes, Lancer," Sarah Jane said, stopping only to sip her already prepared coffee. "You should feel honored because she is very particular as to whom she serves them to."

Lancer quickly put a taste of the cake into his mouth.

"Very particular," Elmira said sternly.

"Hmm, I do declare Miss Elmira, if these aren't the best sweet cakes I've had in a quite a long time," the guest stated. "I'm very pleased you allowed me to taste them."

It was at that moment he remembered the Turkish Delight he brought with him. It was in the saddle bag Lincoln was standing beneath. He thought about going to get it but it did not seem appropriate. He thought he'd maybe perhaps see how the conversation went and save it for another time.

Elmira smiled as she walked away to leave the client and employer to talk business. It was Sarah Jane's cue to start talking.

"Now down to business Lancer as I would like to get matters rolling as soon as possible," she began. "About my husband of course."

"Yes of course, Mrs. Paulson," he replied.

She made no attempt to allow him to address her common. He figured right away she was either going to keep this very professional or she was putting on airs. Only time would tell.

She went on to explain how her husband had been under a great deal of stress for some time. She did not have a clue as to what was happening as he never confided his business interests to her. He was seen in the company of two men, two men she did not know, the day he disappeared. At some point he went to the bank and shortly thereafter rode off with them. He was never heard from again.

"This was the story you told to the sheriff?" Lancer asked.

"Yes."

"Did your husband have any enemies?"

"None that I know of," she answered. "People in business usually have some, but I didn't know of any, and everyone loved Henry. I don't know why anyone would want to kill him."

She began to cry and pulled out a handkerchief to wipe her eyes.

"Well, we don't know that he's dead?" Lancer asked pointedly.

Sarah Jane paused for a moment and wiped her eyes before looking back at Lancer.
"Well, no, of course we don't, but it's just been so long."

Lancer got up and, selecting a handkerchief from his shirt pocket, sat next to Sarah Jane and offered it to her. She took it, head down, weeping. Lancer couldn't help but think the tears were not for real, but he reserved judgment for now.

The air was shattered by the shrill voice of Miley as she entered the room like a brisk wind.

"Dry up those tears girl, there ain't no weeping in that soul," Miley said in a harsh manner. "And who is this, your hired man?

Lancer moved from the sofa to an upright position in front of the old woman. She sized him up as he was sizing her down. Shortness of height was no softening blow to the powerful punch she carried in her pint sized body. Hers was enough to make any man uneasy, but Lancer rolled with it and his charm moved to the forefront.

"My name is Lancer, Mrs. Miller and I presume you are the mother of this handsome yet worried woman on the sofa?"

Miley looked him up and down.

"Is there a last name attached to that handle mister?"

"No ma'am, I just go by Lancer."

"Never trust a man with only one name is what I always say," Miley shoved out as she whisked past him on her way to a seat near the fireplace. "Learned that from my daddy many a year ago."

Lancer's eyes followed her as he twisted his body to trace her every move. Sarah Jane was a distant memory for the moment.

"I assure you madam, I am to be trusted, and if I'm right you are as interested as I am in finding out what happened to the missing Mr. Paulson," his voice assuring Miley of his intentions.

"You mean the late Mr. Paulson?" Miley offered up.

"Late or still alive, I intend to locate what happened to him and those who may have taken him to where ever he resides now," Lancer said. "Be it in a grave or in a cave, or maybe just hiding out somewhere waiting for some lucky person to find him and bring him home. Isn't that right, Mrs. Paulson?"

Sarah Jane, now sitting upright on the sofa tears dried up, had few words to answer.

"I'm hoping you can Mr. Lancer."

Miley seemed assured after their brief conversation but she wasn't holding out much hope for her son-in-law. She didn't trust her daughter and she certainly didn't trust the lawyer she was so friendly with. Miley didn't trust many people but she liked the cut of Lancer's jib. She'd trust him for now and the look she gave him reassured him she was on his side. As long as he didn't step across the line. That line to her was money and family. Lancer wasn't the type who would cross either.

"Now Mrs. Paulson, there was, I understand, a substantial amount of jewelry and cash that disappeared with you husband," Lancer began his query again.

"Why yes, but how did you know that?" Sarah Jane seemed startled.

Miley was happy at her response. It seemed Sarah Jane had met her match in Lancer.

"That's because he knows what he's doing, dearie," Miley offered up. "Is there a problem with that?"

"No of course not, mother," Sarah Jane shot back. "It's just I wasn't prepared to hear that this information was common knowledge."

"I wouldn't say common, Mrs. Paulson, but widely known enough that it was pretty easy information to obtain. Now I've heard about $50,000. Is that correct?"

Sarah Jane got up clutching her hands to her necklace. She didn't want to offer up any further information but she knew if she didn't Lancer would throw suspicion on her, and she didn't want that even more. She sauntered over to the window and stared out.

"In round figures, I guess you could say $50,000 was a good number," she replied.

Miley was astonished. This figure was more than she ever imagined and she quickly got up and moved to face her daughter.

"Fifty-thousand dollars?!"

Miley grabbed Sarah Jane by the shoulder and spun her around. The small woman pulled with all the fury within her. Sarah Jane spun like a top and fell back into a large chair. She was frightened and her mother was looking down at her with rage. Quickly Lancer seized the old woman's arms and held her back, pulling her back toward the fire-place. Elmira came running in to see what the commotion was about.

"What's goin' on in here," Elmira exclaimed. "I's hearing all kinds of noise, you okay Miss Miley?'

Lancer stood as peacemaker in the middle of the room assuring Elmira there was nothing to fear as long as he separated the two related women. He wondered how on earth a mother and daughter could be so at odds as to almost want to kill each other. Who were these people?

"Everything is fine Elmira," Lancer remarked. "Although you might want to bring out some of that very cool lemonade you have back in that kitchen. It might help bring some temperatures down."

Elmira laughed at the suggestion and immediately began liking Lancer. It was the first time she'd ever seen a man take charge of these two women and put them in their place. Elmira felt like danc-

ing. She scooted back to the kitchen in high spir-
its.

"Now look you two, if I'm ever going to do my
job I have to have cooperation from both of you,
you hear me, both of you," Lancer yelled sternly.
"You two have got to work together here, c'mon
you're supposed to be mother and daughter.
Where is all that love you're supposed to have?"

Sarah Jane got up from the chair and straightened
herself out before addressing Lancer's concerns.

"Love?" That went out the window when my
brother disappeared.

"He didn't disappear, he was driven off by you,"
Miley fired back. "First my only son and now your
husband. Can't you get enough!? Can't you stop
your destructive ways? You not only kill men, you
destroy them. Same as your father. Drove him to
an early grave."

"Daddy went to his early grave because of you,
not me," Sarah Jane ripped back at her mother.

Again Lancer had to separate the two from going
at each other. This time he threw the old woman
onto the sofa and her daughter back on to the large
chair. As he stood in the middle of the room he
surveyed the situation, and then decided to leave.

"There isn't enough money in the world for me to
tackle this case and the two of you," Lancer admit-
ted. "Mrs. Paulson, I'll return your retainer in the
morning to Mr. Lovling. I'll keep my expense
money but tomorrow I'm going home to Tomb-

stone. Life is much more peaceful there. Now I bid you good day."

Lancer walked out leaving the two women, mouths agape and Elmira standing at the doorway watching him go. As he got to his horse he reached into his saddle bag for the box of Turkish Delight.

"Girl, come on out here, I have something for you," he said pointing to Elmira.

She followed his command.

When she reached him he handed her the box of candy and she smiled as if she knew what it was.

"Turkish Delight, Elmira," Lancer said calmly. "One of my favorites."

"Mine too Mr. Lancer and I haven't had any in a long, long time," she smiled back. "Mr. Paulson, rest his soul, would bring some home every once in a while. I'd sneak a piece from the pantry and I knew he knew I did it, but we both knew he didn't care."

Before he boarded Lincoln, Lancer queried Elmira.

"Your Mr. Paulson?" He asked. "You liked him didn't you?"

"Oh, yes sir, he was a fine man," she responded. "Don't know what he ever see in Miss Sarah and they was like oil and water. Fighting all the time."

"Over what?"

"Money mostly. He say she got it and won't spend it, she say he don't have it cause he's always spending it. They was just awful to each other sometimes"

Lancer got up on his horse but looked down for one last question.

"You think he's dead Elmira, your Mr. Paulson?"

"Oh I don't know sir," she answered back. "I think he might be, but he wasn't too resilient, kind of a soft man at times when it came to manly stuff, but he had a hard head for figures, when it come to business. But not the kind of man you want leading a wagon train out west."

CHAPTER EIGHT

Lancer was resting on the bed in his room contemplating what might be his last night in Prescott.
Suddenly a knock on the door startled him. He
could tell by the knock it was probably a woman.
Was it Sarah Jane come to apologize? Not likely.
Was it Miley Miller hoping to convince the man in
black her son-in-law was worth looking for? He
doubted it. It certainly was not Elmira.

He snatched up his gun anyway and cocked the
hammer. He'd had this experience before and it
might not go down so easy.

"Who is it?" He asked in a matter-of-fact voice.

"It's Willie Miller, Mr. Lancer."

A sigh of relief fell over him as he uncocked his
gun, only to just as quickly cock it again.

"Do you have a gun, Willie?"

A giggle came from the other side of the door.

"Yes, I do, Mr. Lancer but I'm not holding it on
you."

Lancer smiled as he opened the door to reveal the
pretty young woman standing before him. Gone
were the blue jeans, boots and hat which earlier
had masked her face. Replacing them was a polka
dot dress and a little extra redness to her lips. She
was a pretty young thing he thought. He wasn't
sure if he should ask her into his room but there
wasn't much choice. Besides as he hesitated she
swept past him quickly, walked over to the win-

dow, looked out and just as fast, she sat down on a chair at the table.

"Looking for someone Willie?"

"Just wanted to make sure I wasn't followed," she answered. "I heard you dropped the case and I wanted to come by and see if I could convince you to stay."

Now Lancer understood the pretty girl replacing the rough and rowdy one. She was a woman, he thought. A young woman, she was trying to learn the ways of a fully grown woman.

"And you thought by coming up here in that pretty little polka dot dress and red lipstick, I'd be inclined to give into your womanly wiles?" Lancer suggested.

"Don't you think I'm pretty Mr. Lancer?"

"I think you are extremely pretty, Willie, or should I call you Wilamena?"

Willie got a coy look in her eye and raised her small breasts to their full potential as she stood up and moved softly to the man in front of her. There was a hungry look in her eye as she stood in front of him, moving ever closer. Her front touched his slightly and she softly grasped his arms as her perfumed skin wafted up his nostrils.

Lancer couldn't help but feel tempted by the little temptress in front of him. Her young breasts were firm and inviting. Her soft skin against his chest as she laid her face against his half open shirt was more than most men could handle.

The sound of the street outside with its cowboys and buckboards faded from Lancer's ears as the young girl quickly becoming a woman raised her head. She closed her eyes and pushed her soft lips up toward his.

Suddenly the older man grabbed her right arm and spun her around. She had no idea what was coming next and her first thoughts were he was going to violently take her and rape her. Fear ran through her young heart. This was not to be because Lancer above all was a gentleman. As he spun her he sat down in the same chair she raised from. He quickly slammed her across his knees. He then proceeded to spank her firm buttocks as he would a small child.

"Now young lady, don't you ever try that again," Lancer sternly spoke below a yell. "You are just so lucky that I'm a gentleman and not some cowboy who would take you and take you and forget you are still a little girl."

Willie screamed and shrieked as Lancer's large hand continued to bruise her ego but not her rear end.

"Stop it," Willie screamed. "Stop it you, you, just stop it."

At that very moment a large woman pushed her way into the door followed by two men. One older man and the other quite the dandy.

"What's going on here?" The old woman asked frantically.

"What should have gone on years ago," Lancer answered as he spun Willie into an upright position. "A little girl trying to play big girl long before her pigtails are fully grown out."

The old woman laughed as did the two men behind her. Willie was too embarrassed to do anything but stand there stammering and pointing her finger at Lancer.

"Mrs. Jamison, if you please, either take this wildcat home or leave her here to finish her business like a lady," Lancer said with a slight laugh. "That is, if she'll behave?"

The old woman smiled while leaning back realizing Willie did have some unfinished business with Lancer. Mrs. Jamison looked at Willie with a keen eye.

"Well girl what do you say?" she said, looking at Willie who was rubbing her bottom. "Can you behave in the presence of Mr. Lancer, or do I have to call the sheriff to escort you home?"

Willie looked around at everyone and abruptly folded her arms and sat down in a chair.

"All right, I'll behave, but I won't like it."

Mrs. Jamison smiled at Lancer and shooed the other men away, closing the door behind her. Lancer meanwhile poured the girl a glass of milk and put out some Turkish Delight for her to sample. At first Willie refused but the allure of the soft candy with the powdered sugar on top was too much to pass up. First one, then another and going for a third before she finished the second put the power into Lancer.

"Slow down girl, slow down," he remarked. "You can have them all but one at a time. Now drink your milk and tell me what this is all about."

Willie smiled and gulped and then swallowed the entire glass of milk in three seconds flat to the amazement of Lancer who wondered about the last time the girl had eaten. He walked over to the horn on the wall. It was a direct link to the front desk. Lancer blew into it and the desk clerk picked up right away.

"Yes Mr. Lancer?"

"Would you have the kitchen send up a couple of steaks, some mashed potatoes, some cornbread and butter and a pot of coffee and a pitcher of milk?"

"Yes Mr. Lancer."

"Oh, and would you have them send up some of that new dessert I saw on the menu, ice cream?"

"Why certainly Mr. Lancer, coming right up."

Willie smiled. She had heard of ice cream but never had any. And a steak right now was going to be great.

"Willie, what's this all about?"

Willie went on to explain she didn't want him to leave because that would mean her aunt would win and she believed Sarah Jane was hiding something. Willie said when her grandmother came home and told her Lancer was leaving the case behind, her grandmother wasn't too happy.

"She felt you were the right man for the job, the right man to find my uncle and…"

"And your father?" Lancer cut short her sentence.

"I know he didn't leave us Mr. Lancer, you gotta believe me, he wouldn't do it," she pleaded on the verge of tears.

"Don't worry Willie, I wasn't leaving."

"But you…

"That was just a way to throw your aunt off the trail," he explained. "I'm not too sure she's quite the lonely widow, but I can't quite put my finger on it. I figured if I dropped the case I might be able to smoke out the real culprits and perhaps find a motive."

Willie broke into a big smile.

"So you're not leaving?"

"No, I'm not leaving."

Willie got up and ran to Lancer and hugged him for all she was worth just like the last time. This time though it was the hug of a little girl living for hope and not the hug of a young woman looking to ply her not yet developed womanly wiles.

"You know Willie, you are going to make some man a wonderful wife someday and I'm sorry to say I was just too old for you," Lancer smiled big. "You were pretty tempting and for a moment there I thought about giving in, so don't ever do that again."

Willie pulled back and smiled up at him.

"Don't worry, I won't," she replied. "A wife? Yuck, who wants to be a wife?"

They both laughed as someone knocked on the door. As the door opened it revealed two trays full of food. Willie's eyes lit up wide.

"Willie, when was the last time you ate?"

"Well, if you must know, I ran away from home right after my grandmother told me about you."

"That was more than a day ago!"

"I'm sure she's out looking for me now?"

The waiters brought the trays in and set them down on the table. Lancer gave them each a $20 gold piece as they left. The two sat down to eat their dinner and Lancer made Willie promise she was going straight home after dessert which Willie devoured first. Lancer fondly remembered a time when he was about Willie's age and dessert came first, and went away just as quickly.

CHAPTER NINE

A chat with Sheriff Jackson brought good news to Lancer's ears. Henry Paulson evidently had a lot of hands in a lot of places. If it wasn't a land deal it was a floating poker game. And if it wasn't spending time with Sarah Jane it was keeping time with any one of several young ladies who liked a good time as much as Paulson did. The one thing Lancer didn't figure on was a mining operation.

It seems Paulson bought into an old mine a few years ago with the promise of gold. At the time Paulson was first beginning to feel the daggers Sarah Jane could stick anywhere she wanted. Her long nails were just the tip of the long arm she stretched wherever she wanted to poke it. Paulson decided for the first time he was going to invest his own money into something Sarah Jane couldn't touch. The mine a few miles outside of Prescott could be the very thing to set him up on his own.

Sheriff Jackson agreed to ride out to the mine with Lancer so he could get a feel for what the land-scape held. Prescott was in a valley surrounded by beautiful mountains and those mountains were proven to be treacherous. If it wasn't a snake in the grass it might be a snake on horseback. There had been a spate of robberies outside town and a couple of highwaymen were suspected of pulling them off. No stages in recent months, but these seem to be small jobs with travelers getting held up. No violence but Jackson was concerned. His offer to ride along was gladly accepted by Lancer.

The two rode leisurely about a mile out of town when Lancer noticed something in the bushes off to his right. It looked like a piece of silk cloth, but not the kind to be a part of a woman's dress. It was unusual for something like that to be out there on the trail. The rider pulled up on Lincoln's reins and moseyed over to the unusual silk. He dismounted while Sheriff Jackson wondered what the man in black was up to.

"This look strange to you sheriff?" Lancer asked.

"Looks like a piece of cloth to me, what's so unusual about that?" Was the immediate reply.

Lancer quickly learned the red silk was tied around the bush. It had been put there deliberately for some reason.

"No one just ties an expensive piece of silk to a bush without a reason," Lancer pointed out. "This was put here as a marker or something to mark the trail and since this is a well-traveled trail not far from town, I'd say it was left as a message."

The sheriff nodded in agreement and quickly took what Lancer was saying as fact.

"Let me see that a little closer," Jackson said reaching out.

He inspected it closely and then put it up to his neck.

"I'd be right in saying it looks like a neck tie, Mr. Lancer," Jackson stated.

"Anyone you know wear expensive ties like that?"

"Only two people I know of," Jackson said with assurance. "A lawyer named Lovling and Henry Paulson!"

"Paulson?"

"Yup, the very same man we're looking for," Sheriff Jackson replied.

Lancer rubbed his chin and took the silk back to take a closer look. He noticed the tie was ripped and worn, mostly likely from being in the elements. He couldn't notice any distinguishing marks except it looked a little odd for a common tie.

"This doesn't look like such an ordinary tie though, rather something personal, unique, wouldn't you say?" Lancer asked.

The sheriff shrugged his shoulders as he wasn't an expert on ties and was quite surprised Lancer was.

"Sort of a strange hobby of mine, Jackson, ties that is," he answered. "I'll have to think about this one for a while."

Up in the hills above the pair sat two men on horseback. Keeping the sun at their backs, they hid behind the rocks. They stayed out of site from the lawman and Lancer. The two horsemen watched intently as Lancer stuffed the silk into his shirt pocket and then rode off with Sheriff Jackson in the direction of the mine. As they did, the watching pair followed at a safe distance.

Unaware of the two horsemen trailing them, Lancer and Jackson continued on their way. The tie, or piece of silk clothing, bothered Lancer more than Jackson, although the sheriff knew this was a clue he could not ignore. If it was Henry Paulson's why did he leave the marker? If it was Lovling's what could this mean about his involvement in Paulson's disappearance?

As the pair approached the area around the mine all they saw alerting them to their destination was a broken sign stating "PL Mining Company, No Trespassers."

"P-L," asked Lancer. "I figure the P stands for Paulson. Could the 'L' be Lovling?"

"Don't rightly know," the sheriff replied. "I never looked too deeply into it."

Lancer looked somewhat disgusted at his lawman friend. A lawman, he thought to himself, should be checking all the angles. Then again Henry Paulson had only been missing a few weeks and his wife did have to hire a private party to find him. That should have been his first understanding of what Sheriff Jackson was willing, and not willing to do.

The two dismounted and headed toward the entrance of the mine. Once at the entrance they saw the mine was totally shut down. Rocks were piled high into the entrance about 10 feet inside and there was evidence this was not a natural occurrence.

"Explosives, I'd know that smell a mile away," Lancer said, taking a whiff of the air coming from inside the mine. "Looks like someone wanted to seal this off and seal it for good."

"It'd take an army of men to get into that mine now."

"An army is what you may need sheriff if indeed you want to find the whereabouts of one Henry Paulson."

"You believe he's in there?"

"I wouldn't be surprised," Lancer fired back. "I'm hoping I'm not as surprised about who put him there."

Then two shots rang out from high above. The shots barely missing Lancer and Jackson. The two men dove behind a water trough a few feet away and hid from whoever was firing at them.

"You still think he's not buried there sheriff?" Lancer said with a stern voice.

Sheriff Jackson pulled out his gun and fired off two rounds. He knew Lancer was likely right and he didn't like the situation he was in. Lancer fired off two rounds himself, hitting the rocks near where the shots were coming from.

"What do we do now?" The sheriff questioned.

"You stay here and I'll try to work my way up around the side to get a better look at what we're up against," Lancer said before running off. "Cover me."

Jackson fired several shots in the direction of the gunmen as Lancer scurried off alongside the mine shaft. He could see a catwalk which led above the mine. If he could get up there without getting killed he'd have a decent chance to get into a position to get off some good shots. He might be able to pin the shooters down and give the sheriff a second shot at justice.

As Jackson kept firing, Lancer made his way up the catwalk. At the top step he laid spread eagle, keeping low to the ground. Once Jackson squeezed off a few more rounds, Lancer made his way into the bushes and behind some rocks. He hadn't heard a shot from the opposing side in a few minutes. Had Sheriff Jackson gotten lucky? Were they dead? Or were they waiting for Lancer to appear in the open and give himself away? He wasn't about to do that.

Lancer worked his way up behind the spot he believed the shots came from. In the distance he could see a cloud of dust. Two horsemen were riding rapidly away. Lancer realized quickly they were too far away for his handgun to do any good and his rifle lay strapped to Lincoln's side.

He moved closer to where the original shots were fired from. There he spotted an open space behind some rocks. Cartridge shells were spread on the ground, and he knew the end of this battle had come.

"Sheriff Jackson, hold your fire!" Lancer yelled at this top of his lungs, while waving his arms in the air. Jackson immediately recognized Lancer and held up.

"You okay Lancer?" The sheriff yelled back.

"They're gone, fled on horseback," was his disappointed reply.

Lancer gathered up the shells as evidence and made his way back down to Sheriff Jackson and Lincoln. The long walk back was not as exciting as the run up the hill. Lancer thought of his days in the recent War Between the States and realized he had once again made a charmed escape. Better shots would have put him in the same grave perhaps as Henry Paulson. His time however, had not yet come.

"Did you get a good look at them?" Sheriff Jackson queried, as Lancer approached.

"No, I didn't, unfortunately, but I did get these?"

Lancer showed the shells to Jackson who took them in his hand.

"Winchesters?" The sheriff questioned. "So what?"

"Look closer sheriff, those are Winchester 73 shells, not your standard run-of-the-mill rifle shells," Lancer pointed out minor differences which would determine the shells to be made a decade earlier. "These are extremely rare and whoever took those shots at us should not be hard to track. I suggest we head back to town. The army will have to wait."

Assured their assailants were long gone and not coming back, the pair rode at a quicker pace back to Prescott. As they arrived in town it was about dinner time.

"Can I treat you to a steak, Lancer?" The sheriff asked. "Been a pretty long and eventful day."

"Thank you for your hospitality but I think I need to see a lady about a tie, a red silk tie."

"Let me know what you find out," Jackson answered. "And I owe you one."

Lancer tipped his hat and headed toward the Paulson home across town, while Jackson strode toward one of the better eating places in Prescott. Lancer had bigger fish to fry. He was curious about the tie.

As he rode up to the front of the Paulson home Lancer couldn't help but notice the sun still shown bright in the western sky. It was late spring and the flowers in front of the Paulson home were in full bloom. While tying Lincoln to the hitching post, out of the corner of his eye, he caught the curtains open quickly and just as quickly close again. Sarah Jane Paulson was watching.

A knock at the door and Sarah Jane took the time to spruce up her clothes to make herself look presentable. She pinched her cheeks to red knowing that a gentleman caller was standing at the door. A gentleman she did not expect to see again. Standing half a room away, Elmira got a disgusted look in her eye as she moved toward the door to answer the knock.

"Why Mr. Lancer, we sure didn't 'spect to see you agin?"

"Well, Elmira, I wasn't sure I was coming back," was the reply. "Is Mrs. Paulson at home?"

Elmira opened the door wider and pointed in the direction of the parlor where Sarah Jane stood; trying not to show she knew the man was on his way. As he approached she acted as if she barely cared. Lancer knew better but played along.

"Well, Mr. Lancer, I do declare, are you still in town?"

"Yes Mrs. Paulson, I had a few errands to run before I left so I figured I'd make a stop back here to clear up a few things in my mind," Lancer plodded along. "There were a few things I was rather curious about."

Sarah Jane moved over to the sofa and sat down but barely looked at the man who stood before her, preferring instead to show she shared little interest in what he had to say. Her eyes may have been looking afar out the window, but her ear was keen to his every word.

"There is a mine outside of town, the PL Mining Company Mine," he suggested. "Do you know of it?

"I believe my late husband mentioned he had a share in a mine, but that was his affair and I know little of his business dealings," Sarah Jane responded, putting on more airs than Elmira thought possible. Elmira listened from the other room intently.

Lancer sat down across from Sarah Jane in a lone overstuffed chair facing the left side of the mantle. As he prepared his next words he couldn't help but notice a photograph of a group of men, a team, on the bookshelf to the left of the mantle. He stared for a moment almost forgetting his words. Sarah Jane, noticing the gap in his conversation, looked intently upon him and wondered aloud what the problem was.

"Mr. Lancer, is there something wrong?"

Lancer kept staring at the photo more intently now.

"What is it Mr. Lancer?" Sarah Jane pushed, her voice straining a bit.

Lancer could not believe his eyes. He thought previously Sarah Jane might have had something to do with her husband's disappearance but now he was sure of it. He got up and moved to the photo. It was a photo of the Oxford Rowing Team, clearly labeled. He picked it up and held it in his hands before turning to Sarah Jane.

"Mrs. Paulson, this is an unusual photograph," he suggested.

Sarah Jane got up and moved to Lancer and they jointly held the framed photo.

"Yes, it's the Oxford Rowing Team of 1880," she offered. "Henry's nephew was a member of that team. There he is. He was the assistant captain."

"Were they close?"

"Henry and his nephew?" She responded. "Quite close. They exchanged gifts at Christmas in fact. Henry was quite sad when he drowned last year. It was an accident. It took him some time to get over the fact such a young man was dead. Such a waste."

Lancer put the photograph back on the shelf and moved to the center of the room, where he picked up his hat and started toward the door. Sarah Jane was quite shocked he was leaving so quickly, and before asking any questions about the mine.

"You had some other questions, Mr. Lancer," she reiterated. "About the mine perhaps."

"No, no," he responded. "That's all for now."

He reached for the door handle and turned around again to face her.

"There was one question regarding that mine," Lancer said as Sarah Jane's eyes lit up. "Who was the 'L' part owner?"

"I don't know," she answered. "I told you it was Henry's business and his partners were his business too."

Lancer picked up his hat and left, leaving Sarah Jane to wonder what Lancer came for and what he didn't leave with, or did he?

CHAPTER TEN

It was late in the day and Lancer knew Sheriff Jackson would most likely be in his office preparing to make his rounds. Prescott was growing, but it wasn't too big for the local sheriff not to check the doors of the local merchants. He'd be sure to stop in and check on most of the local bars as well. Of course, he'd have his deputy, Landry Smith; take over some of those duties.

Lancer had not yet met Smith and he didn't have much to go on regarding the younger man. He heard about Smith from his conversations on the trail with Jackson. Smith was about 25 and an aggressive, smart lawman. He'd had some schooling beyond the local education, but he never finished college. He said it didn't interest him.

As Lancer rode up to the sheriff's office he could see the lantern inside lit up the place. The shadow of a slender figure could be seen through the window. It must be Smith because it certainly was not the portly Jackson. The music was playing loudly from several of the nearby saloons and it was often not distinguishable because of the overlap. You might sort of hear "Camp Town Ladies" but "Sweet Betsy From Pike" would probably drown it out from the other saloon down the street. Prescott was a thriving place for sure.

Lancer tied Lincoln to the post out front and made his way into the sheriff's office.

"How do you do, Mr. Lancer?" The casual question posed by Smith.

"How do you know me?" Was the queried reply.

"I think almost everyone in town knows you by now, sir," Smith answered. "You've been out to see Sarah Jane Paulson a couple of times, and Elmira and Miley Miller are both in women's sewing circles."

"You mean gossip circles."

"Ain't that the truth," Smith said with a laugh. "Anyhow, what can I do for you?"

Lancer wandered over to the window and looked out before settling down in a not-too-comfortable chair. He took off his hat and straightened his gun belt to sit more comfortably. He looked up at the deputy to size him up.

"Is the sheriff around?"

Lancer had been around long enough to know not everyone, even those wearing a badge, could be trusted early on. He had a sixth sense about him. The gunman understood one thing above all else; never lay your cards on the table until you must. And he wasn't about to share what he had gained at Sarah Jane Paulson's home with anyone but Sheriff Jackson.

"He's making his rounds," Smith replied, backing off just a bit. "Should be back soon though if you care to sit a spell."

Smith was taken aback by Lancer's obvious lack of trust. He also knew if Lancer was being coy it was because the gunslinger had some bit of information which must be important. Important enough not to share it.

Smith was a young man for sure but he was older than his 25-year-old frame. Smart, good looking and unwed, he was a catch for any woman in town. Lancer wondered about the young man. He knew quite a bit about the Paulson household women. Reality would say that wasn't too hard. Rich folks, sewing circles and a missing husband after a missing brother. All too scandalous for a gaggle of old hens to keep out of the gossip circles. Still, there was something about this young lawman which just didn't sit well with Lancer.

"You learn anything new Lancer?" Smith sought out. "I mean about Henry Paulson's disappearance."

"Sheriff tell you anything new?"

"Just the two of you went riding out to that old mine they kept and you had a little trouble," Smith offered back.

"Two gunmen firing rifle shots at our heads is a little more than a little trouble deputy, don't you think?"

Smith nodded in agreement then looked out across the street to see Sheriff Jackson striding toward the jailhouse. He pointed in the general direction of the street to get Lancer's attention. Lancer knew straightaway his conversation with Smith was over. His conversation with Jackson was about to begin. He wanted to make sure Smith wasn't in earshot.

A broad smile appeared across Sheriff Jackson's face when he entered the door.

"If you've come to take me up on that dinner Mr. Lancer, I'm afraid you're too late," the sheriff grinned. "I already et supper and the steak was pretty damn awesome."

"No sheriff, you still owe me that, and I'll take you up on it at the appropriate time, so you are not off the hook," Lancer said with a grin. "I've come to discuss another matter with you."

Jackson's smile immediately turned to concern because he knew the gunslinger was working this case to the end. Jackson urged Lancer to tell him what he learned. Lancer however was not about to talk in front of Smith. It wasn't that he didn't trust Smith; it was that he didn't trust him just yet. As Smith listened more closely, Jackson caught the look in Lancer's eyes and knew right away the conversation about to take place would only be between the two of them.

Jackson looked over at Smith and without much ado informed him there was more to do on the street.

"Give us a minute will you, Landry," Jackson said with an authoritative tone.

Smith was instantly taken aback, but a stern look from Jackson meant the order would stand.

"What can he say about this case that I can't hear?" Smith fired back with an angry tone aimed at Lancer. "I'm a hired deputy, he's a hired gun-slinger."

"Landry, what Mr. Lancer has to say he wants to say to me," the sheriff said firm but with a bit of anger. "Now when I give an order to the hired deputy I expect it to stand."

Smith wasn't too happy and stood face to face with the sheriff, but not budging.

"Look deputy," Lancer said softly. "It's not that I don't trust you, okay, it's not that at all. It's just that the sheriff and I here, well, this is something pretty sensitive and the fewer ears that hear it the better. No matter your position in all of this, loose lips do sink ships."

Smith was cooled a bit, but not enough to stay to-tally calm.

"I'm not happy about this sheriff," Smith offered in a little softer tone. "Not happy at all, but I'll do as you say."

With that Smith grabbed a rifle off the wall and walked briskly out the door. A saloon would be his first stop and not likely his last.

The sheriff meanwhile turned to Lancer with im-mediacy.

"Now, what's so damned important that you had to piss off my deputy?"

Lancer mulled over the situation and then pulled the red silk tie out of his pocket. He laid it on the sheriff's desk, but Jackson was not impressed enough to respond.

"Sheriff, remember I told you there was something about this red silk tie that I found interesting?"

"I do, but what's this all about?"

"In 1880, the Oxford Rowing Team wore red silk ribbons on their caps during competition," Lancer responded. "At some point they chose to make those red silk ribbons into ties. They were honoring their school and only members of the rowing team would have them, and have access to them. They were important enough to make newspapers around the country."

The sheriff was still not convinced and motioned Lancer to go on with his story.

"For a member of the Oxford Rowing Team to give up one of these ties would be almost sacrilege unless he was dead. See this marking right here on the tie?"

Sheriff Jackson took a closer look at the mark, which was almost faded away by the sun and the wind because it hung on that bush.

"That marking signifies this came from that very Oxford team. Now while I was at the Paulson home this evening I noticed a photograph on the mantle. It was of that very same 1880 Oxford team. When I questioned Sarah Jane about the photograph she said the assistant captain of that team and in that photograph was Henry Paulson's nephew. A nephew so close to him they would exchange presents at holiday time."

The sheriff sat back realizing the seriousness of what Lancer was saying.

"So you think that silk tie belonged to Henry Paulson?"

"I know it did, and the fact that Sarah Jane didn't point out the tie but ended up telling me the story she didn't want to tell me, means I caught her off guard," Lancer surmised. "She squirmed a bit and had to think quickly on her feet, and that indicates to me she almost definitely is in on it, or at least knows a lot more than she's letting on."

"Did you let on about this?"

"No, of course not, I came directly to you," Lancer offered up. "And I'd like this to stay between me and you until I can figure out where this is going."

The sheriff nodded in agreement now fully understanding the seriousness of the accusation. If Sarah Jane knew about the tie being left as a marker by her husband, it might tip her off as to what the sheriff and the gunman knew, or at least suspected.

"My next stop is the land office in the morning," Lancer pointed out. "Our Mrs. Paulson said she knew nothing about the mine except her husband owned a portion of it. When I asked her about it she didn't say he had a 'partner' but rather she used the plural 'partners,' indicating more than one."

"You think the 'L' partner is a front, or maybe the up front man in a group of silent partners?" The sheriff asked.

"I don't know but I'm going to find out, because I think therein lies the story as to why Henry Paulson is likely buried at the bottom of that mine."

Jackson agreed and urged Lancer to follow up on his lead. He went on to say he didn't get any information yet on the two gunmen who took shots at them. When Lancer asked who else knew about the attempt on their life, he said he had to tell Deputy Smith but that was all. He also told the stage manager because he had to keep a lookout for anyone who might fit the description.

"And like I told you, I told Landry that someone fired some shots at us?"

"Was that exactly how you said it 'someone fired shots?" Lancer asked with concern.

"Yup, that someone had fired shots."

Lancer took the sheriff at his word and put that bit of information into his brain for safekeeping. He wasn't too sure about Landry Smith, and from what he was hearing there might be good reason. They needed to keep a lid on this as the plot was thickening. If Sarah Jane was indeed involved, and if Lovling was Henry Paulson's partner in the mine, or maybe just one of the partners, this was getting very interesting indeed.

CHAPTER ELEVEN

Lancer's thoughts were on the mine as he awoke the next morning. Breakfast in his room seemed to be the best idea as he didn't want to be seen any more than he had to. Eggs, bacon and corn bread went well with coffee and a touch of sugar. Topped off with Turkish Delight it all seemed to fit his palate well. Just the right touch of sweetness to get his juices flowing this morning, he thought.

Lancer came down the stairs quietly. There were already too many people in town who knew who he was and what he was doing. Prescott, for all its progress and show of Eastern money, was still a small town with too many people watching the comings and goings of a stranger. The stranger was becoming less of a stranger than he liked. He was out the door this time before anyone could notice much. Or, so he thought.

Deputy Smith was up early this morning too. He sat in the back of the breakfast room at the hotel with his face hidden by the morning edition of the *Prescott Courier*. Smith wanted to see where Lancer was headed and took a chance the gun-slinger would take breakfast in his room and not in the restaurant, where he might spot the junior lawman. He was right on both counts. The newspaper hid his face from the exiting Lancer, and as Lancer disappeared out the door, Smith could see his moves through the window.

The land office was only one block across town and clearly visible from the restaurant. A worried look crossed Smith's face as Lancer opened the door to the land office and entered. He immediately got up and walked outside. He got close enough to see Lancer inside talking to County Land Clerk, Nathan Ericks. Smith stayed out of sight while Lancer conducted his business.

Inside the land office Lancer chatted up the tall, skinny Swede. Ericks spoke with a bit of an accent. He'd come to this country as a boy from Stockholm and while he lost most of his accent it was hard not to refer to him as Swede. Everyone in town did, and the moniker stuck when Lancer introduced himself.

"Mr. Ericks, I presume?" Lancer asked upon entering the office.

"You can call me Swede," was the answer. "Yah, I am him. What can I do yah for?"

"I'm looking for a land deed to a mine," Lancer replied. "Sheriff Jackson said you'd help me with my research. I'm looking to possibly purchase some land around here and I heard about this mine outside of town. I believe it's the P&L Mining Company."

"Sure, let me look it up for you, Mr. Lancer?"

Lancer was not happy Swede knew his identity, but he was soon realizing how small the town circle was in Prescott. He felt foolish offering up his story about wanting to buy land, and he figured Swede knew enough to keep his mouth shut and his business straight. Swede was a good man but, like so many in Prescott, knew things were not right in the Paulson household.

"Ah, here it is, the deed to the P&L Mine," Swede said.

"May I see that?"

Swede responded by handing over the documents.

Lancer pored over the documents, hoping to see something that stood out. Right up front was the name "Henry Paulson" and, as suspected, "James Lovling, Esq." The lawyer was right there on the deed with Paulson. Alongside them in the fine print was the word "conglomerate."

"Conglomerate?" Asked Lancer.

"Yes Mr. Lancer," Swede responded. "Conglomerate. It is sort of a group of partners who also own a portion of the property."

"Yes, Mr. Swede, I know what it is but who are they?"

"They are most likely silent partners who contributed but who don't want their names associated with the property," Swede answered back. "Their names are kept off the deed by county ordinance, but you can find out if you go through the process of a court order. For that there would need to be a lawful reason for the court to open up the records."

"Such as a crime, a murder perhaps?"

"That would certainly do it, yes, Mr. Lancer," Swede responded with a smile.

Lancer rubbed his chin and thought for a moment as he looked upon the bare green walls of the land office. There might certainly be a crime here and a friendly judge might be willing to open up the documents. That is if he or Sheriff Jackson petitions the court to do so. Of course to suspect a crime a body would have to be found.

"When will the circuit judge be back in these parts?"

Swede thought for a moment, then moved over to the calendar on his wall. He looked closely at his own writing on the calendar and pointed to a date three weeks from today.

Lancer walked over and took a closer look before writing the date down in his booklet. The date would stand out in his mind. He had three weeks to dig on his own but if he managed to find nothing and still stay alive, the local judge would have to do the honors.

"I think I'll pay a visit to one Mr. Lovling Esquire," Lancer said, putting his hat in place and moving toward the door. "Anyone else come to see these documents recently?"

Swede shook his head no, and Lancer took him at his word. He said good day and asked if anyone else inquired about the mine to please let him know. He wanted to solve what he still felt was more than a missing-persons report. He was sure Paulson was dead but he wasn't sure who exactly put him in the grave.

He had several suspects in mind as he moved out the door. There was Sarah Jane and Lovling for sure. The silent partners, whoever they were, could be considered suspect and of course the cowboys he met on the trail with guns blazing. A trip to the local store which sold explosives might be in order. He smelled the faint smell of nitro at the site of the explosion and he'd like to find who sold it to the persons who blew up that mine. No one in his right mind would have brought it from outside and up the mountains. Nitro was too dangerous for that. No it had to be shipped in to a local merchant and only one merchant in Prescott handled it; Cleveland Grover's Emporium.

Lancer saw the Emporium a mile out of town. The store, or warehouse more like it, carried all manner of large items and explosives. The town ordinance designated the type of store Grover owned "a nuisance" and, while necessary, it was dangerous. Lancer would make it his next stop.

As Lancer exited the land office, he didn't see Landry Smith looking from behind the corner of another building. Smith slipped farther behind the corner of the structure so he would stay out of Lancer's eye shot. Lancer had direct intentions. He would head directly for Grover's. Ready as always for action, Lincoln sensed things were happening. Lancer boarded Lincoln and the pair rode off at a gallop.

Smith watched as Lancer rode out of town, then moved swiftly to the land office. Once there he adjusted his clothes so as to appear very casual like when he opened the door. Swede stood inside and moved to his desk, where he had his lunch. His wife fixed him a right nice sandwich with some fruit and a little custard topped with a small piece of chocolate. He smiled as he opened the lunchbox but frowned when the door opened with another customer.

Not that he minded Landry Smith. It was just he had his mouth watering for that little dessert for his sweet tooth. The look on his face when he saw Smith must have told the story because Smith apologized right off.

"Sorry, Swede, didn't mean to interrupt your lunch," he pointed out. "What did Lancer want?"

Swede looked up from eating his sandwich and responded without thinking why the deputy would be inquiring about the facts the gunman wanted. At first, he was not interested in Smith's inquisition.

"Just some information on who owns that old mine outside of town, the P&L Mine," Swede responded between bites.

"What did he want to know?" Smith pressed onward.

Now Swede realized the deputy was seeking more than just casual answers. He put his sandwich down and wiped his mouth, with a little annoyance in his actions. He really wanted to eat his lunch in peace but if the deputy was persisting there must be a reason. Whether a good reason or a bad one, he didn't know. All he knew was the man with the badge must have his reasons. Swede leaned back in his chair.

"And why is this a concern of the law, Deputy Smith?"

Now Smith was annoyed. He was wearing the badge and as far as he was concerned anyone questioning that wasn't a good citizen. He leaned on the desk between them.

"Because it is," Smith said, with a stern tone in his voice hoping to intimidate the Swede. "He's a hired gun, a gunslinger and anytime a gunslinger comes into my town I need to keep an eye on him. No! I want to keep an eye on him. If he has any plans I want to know about it!"

Swede was not an easy man to intimidate, but he knew Smith was pushing him so he gave in. He went on to tell the deputy all Lancer had said including the part about the possible crime which might have taken place. This was of particular interest to Smith, who grew somewhat worried at the thought of a dead Henry Paulson lying in the mine shaft.

"Is that all there is?" Smith questioned further.

"I swear he didn't say anything else, he just thought there might be a crime involved and if there is he'd need to see the county judge when he came round," Swede responded as Smith went face to face with him. "I swear."

Smith backed off with a warning to let him know if Lancer made any other visits to the land office. Swede obliged. Smith walked out, but before he did, he gave one last hard look at the Swede who sat not knowing what to expect. Smith doffed his hat and walked out the door. Swede ran to grab a bucket. His lunch had just been disrupted.

Lancer would approach the office of James Lovling soon, but first a stop at Grover's Emporium was mandatory. He rode Lincoln hard for the short ride out of town. No one living anywhere near town felt any ill-will toward Grover. What they didn't like was the fact one wrong move could set off the entire plant and level the town. Grover's would need to be located a safe distance away, and one mile seemed reasonable.

Cleveland Grover was a large man, larger than most. He stood six foot, seven inches tall, and while there wasn't an ounce of fat on him, he probably tipped the scales at over 300 pounds. No one ever knew, because no one had a scale big enough to weigh him, or the nerve strong enough to challenge him. Grover was one of the nicer men anyone ever met in Prescott, so there seemed little reason for suspicion. He ran a clean business, al-beit a dangerous one. He kept a good eye on his employees and ran a ship-shape shop as they say. Above all he was known as honest, and while he minded his own business, he was well into helping with charity work if called upon.

Lancer and Lincoln approached the sprawling set of bunk house type buildings spread out over a dozen acres a hundred yards back from the main road. The large sign at the road head said "Grover's Emporium and Explosives," with an arrow pointing in the direction of a small hill. The road wound through a short mountain pass and half-way there the tops of a few buildings stuck their gray heads over the Emporium. The gunman understood the need for distance between the establishment and the town but this seemed like overkill. In Tombstone they wouldn't care. In Tombstone one wrong match might put the whole town into the heavens. Lancer smiled at the thought, realizing if it was Tombstone, it wouldn't be heaven the town would find as its afterlife resting place.

A large fence surrounded the property and came neatly together at the entrance to Grover's. An armed guard stood at the gateway. A booth for the guard to rest in was all that stood between the rider and the Emporium. As Lancer approached, so did the guard.

"State your business, mister?"

"To do a little shopping," Lancer replied.

"Shopping for what?"

"Information," Lancer replied. "I'm looking for Cleveland Grover. Where can I find him?"

The guard sized Lancer up and down and saw the silver crossed lances on his holster, as if they was protecting the gun inside. The guard motioned to the first building on the right.

"Drop your gun off over there in that building first and they'll instruct you to where you'll find Mr. Grover," the guard responded. "We don't allow no guns anywhere near the explosives, and I think a man of your learning would understand that."

"I do," Lancer said as he gave a soft kick to Lincoln. "Much obliged."

The guard watched keenly making sure Lancer was headed to the small building. As he did, the guard waved his gun in the direction of the building and a wave came back from another man on the porch. Lancer didn't look back but he could feel the signal being relayed in his bones. He certainly understood the reasons for the control of guns as there had to be way too many explosives in the emporium.

A stop at the building on the right produced another guard who came out to greet Lancer. Lancer was asked inside where he turned over his gun belt and watched it go on the wall behind the heavily armed desk clerk. He was given a hand written receipt so when he returned he could pick up his gun and go as peacefully as he rode in.

"What are you looking for mister and how can I direct you?" The clerk asked.

"Tell me where I can find Mr. Grover, please."

"He'd be down there in the lunch room right about now," was the response. "We have a café right over there. You are welcome to take part. The food is excellent and Mr. Grover subsidizes it so the price is pretty good too."

"Thank you and how will I know Mr. Grover?"

"He ain't hard to miss pardner, just look for the biggest guy in the place," the guard pointed out.

Again Lancer said his thank yous and headed across the grounds to the café where he hoped to get some answers from Cleveland Grover. He thought finding whoever bought the nitro should be easy. Grover's operation seemed sound and secure. Certainly if anyone stole anything from this place it would be extremely difficult to get it passed the guards and onto the road.

The noise coming from the entrance to the café sounded more like a cabaret than a lunchroom. There was music and lots of talk. It seemed Grover really did take care of his employees. As the gunman approached many eyes fixed themselves on him. He didn't stop to look around because a few feet in front of him stood the largest man he'd ever seen. The guard wasn't joking. Cleveland Grover was the biggest man in the room - any room, anywhere.

A mountain of a man he was sharing a beer with a much lower-level employee as both ate what looked to be some sort of gumbo. As Lancer stood and watched, within seconds Grover realized the man at the door was a stranger who needed some attention and he, being the boss, should provide it. He excused himself and walked over to the gunman.

"Mr. Lancer I presume?" Grover asked with a smile on his face.

Lancer nodded with assurance despite being annoyed he was not as inconspicuous as he'd hoped.

"I've been expecting you," Grover added. "C'mon let's head over to my office."

As they turned to go, Grover stopped.

"Have you had lunch yet?" He asked. "My cook puts out a pretty nice spread."

Lancer looked over to the table and saw biscuits, gravy, roast pork and several vegetable dishes, which he had to admit, looked pretty appetizing.

"You make it pretty hard to pass up, Mr. Grover," Lancer replied with a smile.

"Good. Hey cookie! Send a plate for the gentleman here over to my office and a pot of coffee too," Grover said in a loud voice. "One of the hands will bring it over shortly."

The two men walked across the yard to what looked like an office outlet. The words "Grover Enterprises" were plastered on a sign above, with the smaller words "Cleveland Grover, proprietor" underneath. The walk to the building included some pleasantries about how the Emporium was quite a place and how when he came to Prescott, Cleveland Grover was a complete unknown, until he struck it dry with a mining operation.

"A dry hole leads you to think there has to be more to life than digging for gold," Grover told Lancer. "It makes you think you should let someone else do the dirty work and you just sell them what they need to succeed, or fail, if that be the case. Makes for a mighty better life and a rather consistent pay at the end of the month."

Lancer wondered out loud where this dry-hole mine he was talking about happened to be. Grover made no secret of the fact it was the mine eventually sold to Henry Paulson and his partners but he had unloaded it long before that.

Inside the office Lancer sat down with Grover behind closed doors. Grover poured his new found friend a drink of whiskey but pulled it back just as quickly.

"I forgot you're a brandy man, Mr. Lancer, I'm sorry, can I get you a nice glass of my best brandy?" He said apologetically.

"You can leave the whiskey but I never pass up a shot of some good brandy," Lancer replied. "Or any brandy for that matter."

Grover put the drink back down on the table and moved quickly to a locked storage cabinet behind his desk. Unlocking the door as Lancer watched he pulled a slim bottle of darkened liquor from the top shelf, where it was placed as a special selection.

"I think you are going to like this, especially as you are a connoisseur of fine liquor," he said, taking the bottle from the shelf and putting down two more glasses. "This is a 20 year old brandy I had brought over from the Potenza region of Italy. The grapes are grown high in the central mountains and distilled. Some are made into grappa, firewater to be sure, while the finer, more elegant grapes are distilled into a lovely brandy."

He poured the savory liquid into the glasses with care and a large smile. Cleveland was obviously proud to share his love of good brandy with someone who appreciated the same. He could hardly contain himself. Lancer watched in anticipation and when it was topped off, they raised the snifters to the heavens and touched glasses.

"Salute!" Lancer offered the traditional Italian toast. "Ai cuori caldi e notti calde (to warm hearts and warm nights.)"

As they sipped the first drink and both men savored the taste, Grover could not help but be impressed with Lancer's command of the Italian language.

"I'm impressed sir," Grover offered back. "Grazie mille."

"That, sir, is a fine brandy."

"When it comes to brandy," Grover came back. "Only the finest will do. Now I know you didn't come out here to sample my brandy and my food, so how can I be of service?"

"The very mine you once owned may be at the heart of the mystery surrounding the disappearance of one Mr. Henry Paulson," Lancer pointed out. "You may be able to help me on that score."

"Sure but what can I help you with? I sold that mine a long time ago and I believe it's changed hands once or twice since then."

Lancer felt he could open up to Grover and decided to share most of his thoughts on the subject. He explained how he and Sheriff Jackson felt Paulson may indeed be buried in the shaft which had been detonated with nitroglycerine. A fact not lost on Grover.

"Nitro is a difficult thing to move so whoever used it to blow up that mine shaft probably bought it from me," Grover pointed out. "Right here at the Emporium."

"That's what I was hoping to hear you say," Lancer said taking another sip of brandy.

"I'll be able to get that to you in a day or two by going through the records," offered Grover.

Lancer did not tell Grover about the red silk tie nor did he share with him his doubts about the sincerity of Sarah Jane Paulson in her husband's death. He did, however, wonder about the family lawyer and his connection with the mine. It was something Grover knew nothing about. He did offer up he knew Lovling and Henry Paulson were seen often together shortly before Paulson disappeared.

Grover also shared the feeling Lovling had little stomach for dirty work and if he had been involved in getting rid of his partner, if they were partners in the mining operation, he would not bother to let his own hands be involved. He knew enough to stay out of legal troubles and would not be surprised if Lovling actually hired someone else to do the deed.

Lancer figured as much. Most men of the day who wore a suit, carried a briefcase and at the same time carried more weight around their mid-section than they should, usually were on the less than active side when it came to doing the nastier deeds of life. He felt as much about Lovling.

"Politicians?!"Grover fired back. "Lazy men taking everything they can from honest hard working folks."

The word raised an eyebrow with Lancer. The mention of politics was the first he'd heard since his arrival in Prescott.

"Oh yes, you didn't know?" Grover asked. "Mr. Lovling is being touted as a candidate for governor to succeed John Fremont. Not that he'd ever get elected, but there are certain circles looking to push him into the governor's mansion."

"No I did not know that," Lancer thought out loud. "You would think someone would have mentioned that to me along the way."

"Well, it's not widely known outside of certain circles," Grover said. "He's talked to those about it who might be able to help him financially. It's not a cheap proposition to run for high office. He came to me but I'm not a fan. If you talk to anyone with money in this town they've been approached. We were all told to keep it very quiet though as he hadn't decided to run. Certainly that's why I'm sure he kept his close ties with Henry Paulson and Sarah."

Now Lancer was putting two and two together and aside from a few ripples he was beginning to understand where this might be going. Why, however, would Lovling take a chance and get rid of his wealthy partner, possibly creating a scandal? Unless, that is, it was a chance to avoid an even bigger scandal. What could be bigger than murder?

The two men pretty much talked out everything they could on the matter and settled on a second glass of brandy just as one of the hired hands arrived with two trays of food.

"Well this looks mighty appetizing Grover," Lancer said, eyeing the warm biscuits. "Always have a special fondness for warm bread."

Grover smiled as the two munched down for a hearty lunch. Lancer was going to leave with more questions than answers but at least he was going to leave on a full stomach.

CHAPTER TWELVE

The house of Sarah Jane Paulson was quiet on this evening. Miley had gone to be with her sewing circle of friends and Elmira had the night off. Her daughter lived in Cottonwood and was with child. Elmira asked for a few days off in addition to this one night and Sarah Jane granted her request. It was the perfect night for the lady of the house to entertain the gentleman who was coming to call. It was a night he kept as much a secret as he could.

A dark shadowy figure slipped in the back gate and up on to the porch of the Paulson's home. The rear porch was broad and sported a sofa and two chairs with a table for snacking in between. It was the perfect setting for a romantic interlude. However, neighbors were nosey enough to just get a whiff to gossip about. If Sarah Jane had a man in the house so soon after her husband had gone missing, the town society juices would flow.

Sarah Jane heard the footsteps of the man she was waiting for as he stepped on to the porch. She moved to the back door and gently unlocked it. Then she stepped back into the kitchen where she waited for him to provide for her what she needed as a woman.

As she sat there with her back turned to the rear of the house, she gently unclasped the top button of her high collar. He would want to do the honors but she was anxious and gave it a good start. As his footsteps got heavier, approaching the lady he was about to take in his arms, her chest welled up from deep inside. He could hear her breathing heavier as he approached.

His hands only slightly moist as he came closer. His lips were somewhat dry as he anticipated the woman's every move. She knew what she was doing and he liked it that way, but he would have his own way as well. Sarah Jane also liked his strength, and as his hands slipped on to her shoulders from behind, her eyes rolled at his touch. She had been waiting for this moment for days and now he was here. He was touching her.

As he slipped his hands over her shoulders her buttons seemed to disappear. His hands continued to slide down her front, into her tight inner wear to cup the two beautiful breasts which rose to the occasion to meet his fingers. Her nipples grew hard as he gently caressed them. His face leaning over her leaned back head, their lips meeting in passion.

As they swallowed each other's juices and shared only the passion two lovers can share, she rose and turned to meet him. As she did his hands moved up and slid the top off her alabaster white shoulders. He plunged his mouth onto her neck and aggressively took her breath away. Just as suddenly he pulled back, staring into her eyes with wanton desire. The man reached down and lifted her up, carrying her away into the bedroom down the hall where he knew they would be alone for the next several hours. The passion had only begun.

Two hours had passed. As they lay there, exhausted from the incredible experience they had just endured, Sarah Jane looked at her lover. She stared forever into his eyes, caressing his cheek as he laid on his side staring into her deepness.

"I've never had anyone or anything like you, Landry," she uttered. "You are so incredible. Strong but gentle, powerful and passionate. I've never known the passion you unleash upon me."

Landry Smith was much younger than Sarah Jane Paulson but he enjoyed the wiles of the older woman who unleashed her passion upon him. He was staying strong and silent. He knew that if she ever found out he was more impressed with her than she was with him, the mystery in their relationship might come to an end. His strength was in knowing she didn't know more about him. Sarah Jane had been so starved for love for so many years she found the combination of Smith's youth and strength almost too much to handle. However, she was going to handle it as long as he allowed her into his bed.

"I'm a man who loves to play with toys," he spoke softly to the lady he'd just bedded. "And you my dear have the loveliest toys in Prescott."

It was something she normally would have smiled at hearing, especially from a younger man. She had learned to put away toys long ago. Now, however, her look was distant despite her recent passion and joy. She stared off into the remoteness, out the window toward an ever bright moon.

"What's wrong, did I say something wrong?" Smith asked as Sarah Jane sat up on the edge of the bed.

"No, nothing at all," she responded. "My mind is far away at the moment because I don't know what to do about Lancer."

Smith got up and walked across to the basin where he began to wash his face. He took his time, not knowing what to say about the gunslinger who seemed wiser than they both thought. He turned back to his lover, wiping his hands on a towel as he did.

"I still can't figure out why you brought him up here," Smith queried.

Sarah Jane sat puzzled, perhaps wondering the same thing.

"It seemed like a good idea at the time," she said. "If a man like Lancer could find nothing, and everything looked legitimate, things would go easier on us. No suspicion and no entanglements. I didn't think he'd be this good."

Smith took her in his arms and kissed her hard, so hard he almost fell back on the bed with her.

"He's good but he can't be that good," Smith added. "But if he gets close to the truth, he'll have to go."

The lady looked a bit less than horrified at the suggestion. Killing her husband was one thing but to cover it up with the murder of a very popular gunman was quite another. No, if Lancer had to go, it was going to look like an accident. Or, maybe he left town, or perhaps there was another way. Maybe the gunslinger proved too much to stay out of trouble. Maybe something could happen to set him up.

Smith watched as Sarah Jane's eyes lit up and her mind started to twirl about. He knew this look for certain. Something was going on in that pretty little head of hers and while he wasn't sure what she was conjuring up, he'd bet it was a doozy.

"Look," she said. "It's getting late and mother will be home soon. You better get a move on."

"Aw, c'mon, let me in on what you're planning."

"No, not until I figure it out," she answered.

"Let me in on it," he pushed. "Miley won't be home for a little bit and don't you think she knows about us?"

Sarah Jane tried to look shocked at the suggestion but it wasn't working. Miley was sharp and while a good gossip, she never let a good story get in the way of the truth. She probably did know but maybe there was a hint of decency still in her and she was trying to protect her daughter.

She shooed Smith away and pointed toward the back steps in an effort to get him to leave. The moon was full and he'd be easy to spot going out the back door if a nosey neighbor had a mind to. Smith took the hint. He knew when she made up her mind, there was no budging her. He slipped out the back unnoticed and moments later Miley came up the front steps whistling a tune. Sarah Jane pretended to be asleep when Miley came to check on her. The old woman moseyed off to her room and the night went quietly away. It was uncanny, Sarah Jane thought. A murdered husband, an affair with her plotter and she was going to sleep soundly. Who had she become? What had she become?

CHAPTER THIRTEEN

The night was young at the Palace Saloon and Lancer's luck at the tables was pretty good this night. The music got louder and a dance hall girl or two shinnied up to him. When the stack of chips got larger so did their boldness. A gambler's wad was always appreciated by those who were more than willing to take it away from him.

Suddenly a loud drunken noise came through the outside doors and many of the patrons turned to look.

"I'm here to get even with the dirty swindlin' cheat who stole my money and I don't care who knows it!" Beaux Thornton yelled as he held his hands close to the six-shooter on his hip. "Now where is he?"

No one moved for what seemed like an eternity. Thornton looked around for a few moments and headed toward the poker tables. At first he moved slowly, looking over the players and hunting for the man he deemed had wronged him. He gazed upon the table where Lancer held five cards closed in his hand.

"Where is that mangy, gutless dog?" Thornton said, raising his voice.

No one answered as few knew who the drunk was talking about. Among the four players who looked up at Thornton, three showed some fear. Lancer kept his head in his cards, refusing to make eye contact with Thornton. Angered, Thornton ad-dressed the man in black loudly.

"Mister, when I speak in your direction I expect you to look me in the eye," Thornton directed his comments to a non-obliging Lancer. "I said look at me!"

Thornton held his hand over his holstered gun. He was ready to draw on Lancer but still Lancer had no reaction except to look at his cards. The pit boss moved over near Thornton to try to calm him down.

"C'mon Beaux, the man you're looking for left town this morning," the pit boss pleaded. "He left with a lot of people's money, so, set down and have a drink."

"I don't want a drink!" Thornton said angrily. "I want this man to acknowledge me proper."

Still Lancer sat quietly, refusing to look up. The pit boss tried to reach out to the drunk but Thornton quickly pushed him aside. The other players got up quickly and moved from the table but the gunslinger sat his ground. Thornton leaned in with his left arm balancing on the middle of the table. He slowly pulled the gun from his holster and started to put it in Lancer's face.

"I don't see you giving me respect mister," Thornton began.

As Thornton moved his gun steadily closer with catlike quickness Lancer pulled his pistol from his holster with his right hand. As he did, his light-ning-fast left hand dropped the cards and grabbed the drunk's gun hand and pushed it away hard. The gun went off with a shot into the wooden floor. With his right hand, he used the side of the metal weapon and slammed it into Thornton's left temple. The blow was so hard and fast it knocked the drunk to the floor in a state of unconsciousness.

Lancer stood up and took Thornton's gun. Handing it to the pit boss, he holstered his own weapon and stood over the drunk.

"Give it back to him when he wakes up," Lancer addressed the pit boss. "I have a feeling he's going to have a pretty good headache when he comes too."

With that Lancer walked a wide path through the crowd and up the steps toward his room. With him, a hat full of chips to cash in later. Tonight was over and while he'd come close to death, he was only beginning to feel the release from the fear such adrenalin can cause.

The crowd behind him stood quiet as he passed them by. The dance hall girls gained new respect for the man in black. After he left they discussed among them which of them would be brave enough to knock on his door before morning. Lancer would try to sleep softly this night. It wasn't to be.

Six hours later Lancer rolled over to find, to his surprise, a naked woman lying next to him. He only half remembered the knock on his door. Perhaps it was the few drinks he had or maybe the come-down off the adrenalin. Either way he did not remember much of what went on after that.

"Have you been here all night, Miss….?" Lancer asked with a look on his face which said he really didn't know.

"Holly, Holly Woodnite," she answered. "And yes, most of the night as far as I remember."

"Well, I hope it was a pleasant night and that I was a gentleman," Lancer said, with a gentle smile.

"I can honestly say I've never been treated to a better evening and a more pleasant night," Holly smiled back. "All three times."

The look on Lancer's face was one of shock mixed with pride. They looked deeply into each other's eyes and his eyes read surprise as well as pleasure. She smiled back with a nod, as if to say "yes, three times." His smile turned to pure pride and confidence as well as a sense of accomplishment.

Holly slid from under the covers to reveal a beautifully shaped body with long legs leading up to a round dancer's rear end. He enjoyed every movement of her body. Lancer's eyes followed as she crossed near the window to retrieve her clothing.

"You might not walk too close to that window Holly," he said, with caution.

She smiled briefly at him in her coy manner.

"What makes you think someone on that street hasn't seen this before?"

The look in his eye said he was confident he was not the only man she'd ever slept with, but in reality all he had to know was he was the best man she ever slept with. As she finished dressing she came back to lean over him on the bed. She kissed his lips gently.

"You were the absolute best, Mr. Lancer," as she pulled away. "Absolute."

With that she threw her remaining clothes over her shoulder and exited through the door to the hallway. Lancer leaned back on the bed with a smile toward the heavens. As he lay there contemplating where his day would begin he wondered what happened to the cowboy who claimed he was cheated out of his money. He didn't have long to wait for the answer.

A loud knock sounded on the door and he knew it as the knock of a man's fist. His mood changed from pleasure to danger very quickly. Rolling out of bed Lancer reached for the gun still in its holster and stood next to the door frame. He positioned himself where the door would open with him behind it.

"Who is it?" He said, with a stern tone in his voice.

"Breakfast Mr. Lancer," was the response from the voice. It was one of the bell boys.

"I didn't order breakfast."

"Complements of the house, sir," the bell boy answered back.

Lancer slowly opened the door revealing the young man with a tray of food and a newspaper. Lancer crept out to the hallway looking up and down to make sure the hotel employee was alone. The bell boy wasn't sure what to make of the man's actions so he stood by like a statue. He didn't want the gun to accidently go off and ruin breakfast as well as his life. Lancer motioned for him to enter and he did.

"Tell whoever sent this to me, thank you, but," Lancer said, until he was interrupted.

"The pit boss, John Henry, sent it, Mr. Lancer," the bell boy said. "Something about helping out last night."

Lancer now understood as the young man handed him a newspaper and waited for a tip which was gladly provided by the man inside. A smile crossed the bell boy's face as he started to walk away.

"Oh, by the way, whatever happened to that cowboy?"

The bell boy turned and looked with surprise at Lancer, surprised that he had not heard.

"He's dead sir," he blurted out.

Lancer stood dumbfounded with a look on his face that stood for question mark.

"Yes sir, shot while trying to escape the jail last night."

"Shot by whom?"

"Deputy Smith."

Lancer's face grew cold and straight. So cold the bell boy didn't wait around and hurried off. Deputy Smith shot and killed a drunken cowboy for trying to escape? A drunken cowboy who was only a bit out of line and couldn't possibly have been a real threat to escape, if he was put into jail properly. And Smith would have no reason not to put him into jail properly. This plot was thickening and his dislike for the young lawman was growing.

Right now, he was going to try to enjoy his breakfast. He uncovered the tray to see three eggs, bacon, bread, jam, coffee and juice. Off to the side was a small note.

"You've no doubt heard about what happened after you left last night. Contact me."

It was signed "John Henry, Pit Boss, Palace Hotel"

This was going to be an interesting day.

CHAPTER FOURTEEN

Exiting the Palace Hotel and Saloon, Lancer's first stop had to be the jailhouse to see what happened to the cowboy and why Smith shot him. Sheriff Jackson was waiting for him when he arrived.

"I didn't think it would take you this long to get here, Lancer," the sheriff said, when the gunman entered the door. "What kept you?"

"I'd be remiss if I didn't tell you it was a woman?"

"Holly is a pretty one that is for sure."

Lancer was surprised the sheriff knew who he spent the night with. It was becoming a bothersome thing because every time he seemed to turn around, someone knew what he was doing. It was not to his liking but he was learning there wasn't much he could do in Prescott that didn't get noticed.

"What the hell happened, sheriff?"

Jackson went on to explain after Lancer had laid the cowboy low, John Henry called upon the law to sweep up the remains. He, Jackson had already gone home for the night and the messenger summoned Deputy Smith. Smith arrived, calmly took Thornton into custody and placed him in a chair outside the cell until he could get the cell key which he'd left inside the desk drawer.

It seems Smith felt Thornton was harmless enough even though he had come too. As the deputy fished for the keys he dropped them on the floor. As he bent over to pick them up the prisoner seized the opportunity and rushed the deputy knocking him to the floor. He then ran toward the door, which is when Smith pulled his weapon and discharged it, hitting Thornton in the middle of the back. He died instantly.

"This was even though he was drunk?"

"Yes sir, Mr. Lancer, it was," was the sheriff's reply.

"Sheriff Jackson, doesn't it seem odd to you that a drunken man, just barely conscious and sitting in a chair could get the jump on a much younger deputy with a gun in his own jailhouse?" Lancer queried in a strong voice. "Doesn't it just seem a little improbable that he could act with such catlike quickness to bring down Deputy Smith?"

The sheriff put his hand to his chin and thought about the situation before answering non-committal.

"I see what you're saying Lancer but I'd be mighty careful before I'd accuse my deputy of shooting a man in the back for no good reason," the sheriff sounded off. "Mighty careful."

"Slow down sheriff I'm not accusing Landry of anything, not yet, but I'm just saying it seems a bit odd, don't you think?" The gunman tried to sooth the sheriff's obviously hurt feelings.

Jackson backed off and calmed down before offering Lancer some coffee, which he gladly accepted.

"Where's the body?" Lancer inquired.

The sheriff motioned it was in the back room. The undertaker hadn't been by yet but was expected soon. He ushered Lancer into the rear of the building where Beaux Thornton was laid out on the table face down with a bullet smack dab in the middle of his back. The shot was clean and while no undertaker, or coroner, Lancer had some medical training in the military so he wanted to take a closer look.

As he placed his hand on Thornton's pant leg he pulled back slightly. He rubbed his fingers together as if he'd felt something unusual. It seemed oily to him. The spot was not stained like it would be from the type of oil they were pulling from the ground these days. No, it was much lighter and as he held his fingers to his nose, Lancer caught the slightly familiar smell of a hint of explosives. The oily feeling was the same type found in the residue of nitroglycerine. He looked directly at Sheriff Jackson.

"Did this man work for Grover's Emporium by chance?" Lancer asked.

"No, he was a cowhand at one of the local ranches," the sheriff replied. "Came into town several months ago looking for work. But as far as I know he never worked for Grover. Works for Ken Golder."

If he didn't work for Grover then how did he come in contact with nitro? The only thing Lancer could surmise was that he was at the mine where Paulson was believed buried. It had to be within a couple months and that would fit the time frame. If he was, then there was a chance Beaux Thornton was one of the two men who tried to ambush him and Sheriff Jackson while they were out at the mine site. He remembered one of the riders rode a painted horse with a white rear quarter.

"Where is this man's horse?"

The sheriff saw the curiosity in Lancer's look and pointed to the back of the building. The two men walked out the rear door where a painted pony was tied to the hitching post. Lancer walked around to the rear of the horse where the white hindquarter was in full sight. He moved around to the side of the horse and the rifle sticking out of its slot along the saddle. Lancer pulled it out. He was not surprised to see it was a Winchester 73. He hesitated before mentioning it to the sheriff because of his suspicions of Smith, but he knew too the lawman was on his side.

"What is it?" The sheriff asked.

"This horse belonged to one of the men who ambushed us at the mine the other day," Lancer replied. "And there is a bit of residue from nitro on his pants. Those add up to just one thing. This man is partly responsible for the disappearance of Henry Paulson. We need to find his partner."

Sheriff Jackson quickly grasped the magnitude of the situation. In his mind he must have wondered why Thornton met his fate at the hand of Deputy Smith. Jackson would have a word with Smith over the matter, but now he turned his attention to Lancer. The gunslinger had an idea and a background for what was to come. Now they needed to find the other man.

"Sheriff, I hope you don't take this the wrong way, but I'd like to keep this information from your deputy for a while," Lancer said, with a soft tone in his voice. "I mean, if you don't mind, because, well, I'm not sure I trust him."

The look on Jackson's face was at first anger but it soon turned to a softer tone, because he realized Lancer was absolutely correct. If Smith shot Thornton to keep him quiet about something, then he was likely involved. Jackson didn't want to think about that because he liked Smith, but sometimes liking a man and being true to his job, were in conflict.

"I hope you're wrong Lancer," he said. "I like Landry but I do see where you're coming from and, well, I guess holding back the information for a while won't hurt."

Lancer felt good about the sheriff's decision. He had more important things on his mind right now. He felt paying a visit to both Sarah Jane Paulson and James Lovling would be in order. If he got lucky they might be together. He would drop by Lovling's office first. He also had to ride out to Golder's ranch. Maybe Thornton's partner still worked there.

The ride to Golder's ranch was a cautious one. Before he left Prescott the sheriff explained Golder wasn't to be trusted. There was something about him which didn't ring true. He had the biggest spread in the territory and ran about 1500 head of cattle. Other ranchers had complained about missing cattle. All except Ken Golder who seemed to be immune from rustlers.

Riding up to the Bar G Ranch, Lancer felt like he was being watched. He was. Golder employed a lot of cowboys and some of them were nothing more than armed guards. As he approached the entrance to the main property two men rode out to meet him.

"Can we help you, mister?" One of them asked, showing the rifle as an invitation for Lancer not to make any wrong moves.

"Yes, I'd like to see Mister Golder," he answered. "Name's Lancer."

The other cowboy motioned Lancer to follow him while the first one rode behind the man in black. This did not go unnoticed by Lancer who kept a close eye on how close the man would come. Lincoln instinctively kicked back at some point causing the horse behind him to rear, sending the cowboy to the ground. As he did, the man on the ground immediately responded by pointing his rifle at Lincoln.

Like lightning, Lancer's gun came out of his holster and fired one quick round hitting the rifle and knocking it out of the hands of the man on the ground. Then just as quickly he turned to face the cowboy in front of him.

"Don't even think about it," Lancer said as the man's hands rose into the air.

Several horsemen came down upon the three men in rapid fashion as if they were racing to a finish line. An older man spoke boldly.

"What's going on here?" Ken Golder spoke in a stern fashion targeting Lancer.

"My horse doesn't like someone riding up his butt and this man's horse got just a little too close for comfort," Lancer responded in just as strong a tone. "Your man can get up now."

"Tom, Jake get up and to the bunkhouse and mend your wounds," Golder told his men. "Mr. Lancer, sometimes they have a tendency to be too protective. I'm sorry. We try to treat our visitors and guests with a little more respect. Will you accept my apology sir?"

Lancer holstered his six-shooter and sat quietly for a moment in the saddle.

"Thank you Mr. Golder, I do. May we talk?"

Golder nodded and indicated they would both be more comfortable back at the house. Once at the house the others dispersed to their chores and the two men sat on chairs on the long porch fronting the three-story home. A woman brought out cool drinks with a bottle of hard liquor and some sandwiches for them.

"Mr. Lancer I like the way you handle yourself," Golder began. "I could use a man like you around

here. Would you consider coming to work for me?
I'd pay you well. Meet your price."

"I'm flattered to be sure but running cattle and
staying in one place just isn't the life for me,"
Lancer responded. "Ask me in about ten years and
I might change my mind, though."

Golder, a firm-standing gray-haired man with a lot
of history in his face, was somewhat disappointed
as he downed his drink. He wasn't used to people
saying no to him.

"Well, be that as it may, what can I do for you?"

"I'm looking into the disappearance of Henry
Paulson and I'm told you might know a little
about him," Lancer suggested, not wanting to tip
his hand about the dead gunman just yet.

Golder took another drink and explained he knew
Paulson but he never had any dealings with him.
He brushed the notion aside quickly and when he
did he looked away rather than directly into Lancer's eyes. Lancer knew Golder was probably lying
by just the way he answered. However, he wasn't
going to pursue the same line of questioning for
the moment.

"Did you know a Beaux Thornton?" Lancer
changed the subject.

"Sure do, works for me," Golder replied. "Went to
town and as far as I know, hasn't returned. Not a
very conscientious employee, if you know what I
mean?"

It was obvious now that Golder had not heard about Thornton's untimely demise. Lancer inquired about any of the other cowboys in his employee who might be particularly close to Thornton.

"He keeps pretty much to himself, although I've seen him spend more time with one of the cow hands, Billy Tuesday," Golder said as he thought for a moment. "Billy and he would ride into town together a few times. Why is this important?"

Lancer wasn't sure how to handle the situation but chose to speak right up.

"Thornton was killed last night in Prescott."

The look on Golder's face wasn't one of shock and really wasn't surprise either. It was more of matter-of-fact.

"Who did it?"

"Deputy Landry Smith shot him while trying to escape from jail," Lancer responded. "He was there after pulling a gun during a drunken tirade at the Palace. Smith said he knocked him down and ran, which is when he fired one shot?"

"In the back?"

Lancer's face confirmed the fact.

"Coward," Golder said. "I never did like that deputy, let alone trust him. I had dealings with him and Henry Paulson over that mine..."

Golder caught himself in the lie and so did Lancer, but Lancer refused to acknowledge it, pretending to play dumb instead. He got the answer he was looking for. Paulson, Golder and possibly Smith were partners in the mine. What reason could they have for doing away with Paulson? Golder had lots of money. Did Paulson squander it? Golder obviously didn't like Paulson.

"Where is Tuesday now?"

Golder sat dumbfounded for a moment. He couldn't believe he had just offered the one piece of information he wanted most to hide. However, he thought maybe Lancer did not catch it. He had to move quickly on the answer.

"Rode out early today but I'm not sure where," Golder said. "I have a lot of men working for me Mr. Lancer and I don't keep track of their personal lives, unless it affects mine. Although if you're trying to find some of my workers, you might throw the name Mitchell Gatt into the mix. He disappeared about the same time Henry Paulson did."

Lancer got up and thanked his host and asked if he had any more questions, would Golder mind if he called on him again. The answer was, Lancer was welcome any time. The hired gun was armed with new information now and looking over his shoulder as he rode off, his next stop would be the offices of a lawyer who also had something to hide.

CHAPTER FIFTEEN

Lawyer Lovling was leaving his office heading
out for the rest of the day. At least that is what he
told his secretary Molly, who sat just inside the
door. She protected him from many things but
wasn't sure what the old boy was up to. She'd
been a loyal employee and a trusted friend for
many years. After Lovling's wife died they considered a relationship but Molly put a stop to it.
She felt she could not do her job justice and be
involved with her boss. Besides, while she liked
him very much and loved the attorney as a friend,
there were no sparks there. She just did not love
him the way he wanted her to love him and chances are it would have been a rebound anyway.

Lancer rode up to the attorney's office and walked
in.

"May I help you, Mr. Lancer," Molly asked politely. "If you're looking for Mr. Lovling, I'm sorry
he's out."

Lancer struck up a conversation with the attractive
woman who kept Lovling in check. The Lancer
charm was widely known, and he needed information about her boss. He figured, why not try. It
turned out, while she wasn't interested in her boss,
the likes of the man in black plying her with ooz-
ing charm was very much to her liking. She played
him as much as he played her.

"Well, let me see, my lovely lass," Lancer proceeded. "I could use your help in getting some in-

formation Mr. Lovling, I'm sure, wouldn't mind me having."

Molly turned in her chair and approached the gunslinger. She stood just a few feet away as he watched her smoothly approach.

"Now, what would that be Mr. Lancer?"

He raised his nose to the air as she stood in front of him and took in an aroma before smiling back at her pretty face.

"Is that Jasmine I smell?"

"You are very astute with women's perfume, sir," she responded.

"With a touch of Lilac I think, just a pinch to give it that purple air of a hue," he said, the words gushing out of his mouth.

Molly smiled broadly. This was a man who obviously had taste and if he knew the mix of Jasmine and Lilac, he was obviously educated. He could also afford such things and better. She liked him immediately.

"Do you like Turkish Delight, miss?"

"I don't know that I've ever had it," she said. "I've heard of it and I know it sells in some of the higher end hotels but I've never tasted it before."

Lancer looked a little surprised and then raised his finger as if to say, wait a minute. He remembered the box he had in his saddle bag and quickly, while watching Molly's face all the time, moved

out to Lincoln. He grabbed the box and presented it in front of her. He cautioned her there was a special way to absorb the very best of the delicacy.
,

"First, you have to clear your pallet of all that is in your mind from what you have had earlier in the day," he started out. "You don't have to clear it with wine; just a mind clear is fine. Then mentally clear your nostrils so you can soak in the wafting goodness of the aroma the Turks put into every bite."

Molly closed her eyes and did exactly as she was instructed. With her eyes closed Lancer slowly opened the box. The smell filled Molly's nostrils while a big sensual smile came upon her face. She raised her head and as Lancer took a piece of Delight and raised it to her lips. Her mouth opened as he slid it inside with two fingers.

The powdered sugar coating was a taste worth waiting for. She slowly absorbed the candy, spreading it over her teeth and enjoying every moment before it melted in her mouth and slid down her throat. She opened her eyes and a moan came from within her. A broad smile crossed her face. She wanted to reach out and kiss the man in front of her but she dared not.

"Oh that was wonderful, just wonderful," she smiled. "Do you ply all your ladies with this, Lancer?"

He smiled sweetly as she looked deeply into his eyes.

"Now, what is it that you want, sir?"

He told her about the mine, hoping there was some documentation tying Lovling's name to the mine as the "L" on the deed. She explained she did not know of any such mine and certainly nothing with Mr. Lovling's name upon it.

Lancer further queried Molly about the political aspirations of her boss. She explained she knew about the run for governor, but something caused him to take his name out of the hat. It was something personal which she could not put her finger on, but she knew it was disturbing.

"Was someone trying to blackmail him you suppose?" He asked.

"Blackmail is a strong word, but I could see how that would be possible," she offered. "I just don't know what they would use to blackmail him. He has been a scoundrel in the past, that is certain. I don't know if that would be enough to keep a man from higher political office."

Molly thought about the situation and Lancer could see her mind working. There was something she knew, or at least something was going on in her mind.

"There is more isn't there?"

"Did you say the partner in this mine was Mr. Paulson?" She asked.

Lancer nodded the affirmative.

"I saw Mr. Paulson in here discussing something in Mr. Lovling's office with Deputy Landry Smith a few times," she pointed out. "Sometimes the discussion got pretty heated."

Lancer asked if she could remember any of the words used, nevertheless she said it was always near closing time and she had to leave. She tried not to hear what went on when it came to legalities as it wasn't any of her business. Then she thought for a moment that if something were signed between the parties it might be in his personal file.

Molly immediately went to the file drawer and pulled out the Paulson file. There were two of them. One was marked "Paulson Family" in Molly's handwriting. There was a second labeled just "Paulson," which was obviously in Mr. Lovling's handwriting.

"Here it is," she said with surprise. "This is not my handwriting. I didn't place this file."

"May I see that?"

Molly held back for a moment realizing this was a legal document. She wanted to show it but she was a bit hesitant.

"Molly, this is very likely a murder case and what is in that document might detail exactly the lead we need to solve it," Lancer pointed out. "Now you don't want to be shielding a killer now do you?"

Molly slowly handed the file over to Lancer who promptly sat down to look through it. He pored over it for about 10 minutes before his eyes jumped out. He leaned back in his chair and while taking off his hat, he wiped his brow.

"Do you have any coffee, Molly?"

"Why, yes I do, would you like a cup?"

"Yes, I would," Lancer answered. "And if you have something stronger just pour a little bit in. No, make that pour a lot into that coffee."

Molly looked at Lancer for a moment, knowing he had found something substantial. She wanted to ask why, however she figured the coffee might be the best way to get him to speak about it. She poured the cup and pulled a small bottle of whiskey out from behind one of the law books on the shelf. She poured a shot, thought for a moment and poured a second shot before walking over to Lancer.

Lancer obliged her and drank it pretty much straight down. Molly looked on as if to say, "Now tell me what you found out?" Lancer knew the look and felt while he only just met her he could trust her. After all, she had put herself out for him already. She'd gone the extra mile and he was obliged to do the same.

"Did Mr. Lovling ever mention an insurance policy to you, a life insurance policy?"

"Why no, never," Molly replied.

"Well, according to this, it seems Henry Paulson insisted every partner in the mining venture had to have a $25,000 life insurance policy payable to the other partners upon their death," Lancer said sternly. "We have our motive Molly, and once I find out who the other partners are, the supposed silent partners, we will have our killer."

Molly sat stunned finally realizing her boss may be involved in the murder of a well-respected man in Prescott. Her shock ran deep. She almost could not believe he would be involved in something like this, but if he was being blackmailed, anyone could go over the edge. She questioned Lancer about the blackmail possibilities and he expressed the same feeling. A man might do just about anything to protect his reputation and his livelihood, including murder. Lancer was not convinced however, that Lovling was the killer. He was not about to write off Deputy Smith. He'd seen Smith in action, and he wasn't someone he'd turn his back on during a trail drive.

Lancer got up and hugged Molly, who was grateful for what she'd just learned and certainly for the touch of the man she'd learned quickly to admire. He kissed her on the forehead and warned her not to tell anyone what they had just learned. She swore she wouldn't tell a soul. He left quickly and headed back to the hotel to ponder what he'd learned.

The ride across town was eerie for him now. He kept a close eye on every rooftop and every nook and alley. He was a marked man, and while he knew Sheriff Jackson to be honest, one honest lawman in a town of two didn't cut it for him. Still he rode right down the middle of the street in what he would later consider an ostentatious display. Bold was his middle name and while bold often gave way to making sense; it was boldness he felt he needed to show at this moment.

The Palace Saloon was only a dozen yards away, nonetheless he felt uneasy. He'd felt this before, and as he rode up to the hitching post, he made sure Lincoln provided good cover for him. He pulled to the left of the hotel where an alley was close by. Dismounting Lincoln in the shades of dusk he slipped quietly away. Once into the alley, he circled around back to come up through the alley on the right side of the building. There in a distance he saw a figure with a rifle.

He slowly moved his way through as stealthily as he could toward the figure. The person was looking at Lincoln from around the corner of the Palace, waiting and wondering where the man in black was. He'd obviously dismounted. Where was he?

Then with a slight clicking sound of the hammer drawn back on Lancer's gun the figure raised her hands and lifted her rifle high into the air. Lancer took it slowly and placed his gun back in his holster.

"Willie, don't you realize sneaking up on a man with a rifle is going to get you killed?" Lancer said with a stern monotone.

"I wasn't sneaking up, I was waiting for you," the scared girl replied.

"Waiting for me? You could wait inside the restaurant and you wouldn't need a gun to do it. You know where I am staying. Now here, take this gun and don't ever point it in my direction again!"

Sheepishly lowering her head, and close to tears, Willie was ashamed and frightened. She didn't know where to turn, and now the man who had become her best hope was yelling at her, although not with a loud voice. Lancer held her close as his heart melted. How he could refuse this brave little girl?

"Okay Willie, what is it that you came all the way over here to tell me?"

She wiped her eyes and looked up at him hoping she was right in doing what she did.

"I saw that deputy Landry Smith, over at my Aunt Sarah's house the other night," she said softly, the anger building in her voice. "It was late at night and he seemed to be sneaking out the back door."

Lancer was getting the picture now. He believed her but wanted to be sure.

"Are you sure it was Deputy Smith?" He asked. "I have to know you are sure it was him."

She nodded that it was.

"I know what I saw Mr. Lancer," she said convincingly. "It was him. It was very late and my grandmother wasn't at home, at least not yet. I was going over to see her when I saw him. I was scared and waited until my grandmother came home and then I went in."

"And then what?"

"I saw Aunt Sarah looking like she'd, well, she looked like she was messy, not herself," Willie replied. "She always looks so perfect, never a hair out of place. This time she looked like she just got out of bed."

Lancer smiled. Perhaps Sarah Jane had just gotten out of bed but she hadn't been sleeping. Willie was a little young, or perhaps naïve to understand what happened, but it didn't get past him. He asked about anything Mrs. Paulson said, and Willie said no words were spoken between her and her grandmother. It seemed like a very cold moment in time. Miley gave Willie some milk and cookies and sent her on her way home.

Lancer felt it was time for him to do the same.

"Thank you Willie, you've been a big help, now run along home," he encouraged her.

She smiled with the "thank you' comment and kissed him on the cheek before running off. He couldn't help but feel flattered. Now he had business. Entering the saloon he remembered John Henry wanted to talk to him. He side stepped into the casino where the pit boss caught his eye. John Henry waited for a moment and told his blackjack dealer he'd be right back.

The music was loud enough to cover any conversation they could engage in so Lancer felt standing in the casino and talking was good enough. John Henry ordered a couple of drinks just to make it look casual in case anyone got suspicious. He motioned for Lancer to join him near the window.

"Lancer, I just thought I'd let you know, I know you're working the Paulson case, so well, I just want to make sure," John Henry stumbled.

"Don't worry John, this will be kept confidential, so go on," Lancer reassured the pit boss.

With that assurance John Henry went on to tell Lancer how Henry Paulson first bragged about the mine. How he and his partners were going to strike it rich. He never mentioned the partners but he did brag. At some point Paulson started gambling heavier than normal. He was losing large sums of money and had a lot of markers to the casino which are still outstanding.

"How much would you say he owes the house?" Lancer queried.

"I'd have to say it's up around $20,000 at least and maybe more," John Henry replied. "I don't know the extent of it because I only approved certain amounts. The owner approved the others above me."

"The owner?"

"Yes, Harmon Allison, he's a political power broker in the state who lives up in Flagstaff but has business interests all over," the pit boss replied. "Rarely see him, although he was in town a couple of the nights Paulson sought a bigger stake."

John Henry then went on to say there were several arguments between Paulson and Landry Smith. Smith even grabbed him and hauled him out of the saloon on a couple of occasions under the guise he would take him home. Seems Paulson had been drinking too much on these occasions but it seemed odd that Smith took such an interest in Paulson's affairs.

"From what I've learned this night, that is a rather interesting way of putting it" Lancer offered out loud.

John Henry didn't know what the gunman was talking about and wasn't about to ask. Lancer thanked John Henry for his help and decided to call it a night. He stopped at the front desk to check for messages and the clerk handed him an envelope. Lancer opened it to find it was from Sarah Jane Paulson.

"Need to talk to you as soon as possible. Can we discuss it over dinner tomorrow night at my place? SJ Paulson."

What a great idea he thought to himself. Good thing he'd packed his dining clothes.

CHAPTER SIXTEEN

His gray suit fit his trim body perfectly. Walking down the steps from his room into the lobby of the Palace Hotel, Lancer turned far too many heads to count. The striking figure of a man wearing a suit made in Boston was just too much for the women of Prescott to bear. One woman tripped over a spittoon, as she did and Lancer had to quickly come to her rescue. She didn't seem to mind him breaking her fall with his strong arms.

Lancer tipped his hat and without a smile proceeded out the door. He wasn't wearing his gun belt, but the small caliber .22 handgun he kept tucked in his shoulder holster would prove a point in any fight. He didn't like not carrying his perfectly balanced pistol when he was working a case. It was even more important since it was Sarah Jane Paulson with whom he was dining. It didn't seem right to take such hardware with him. The secondary weapon would be his insurance. Besides, he always had his derringer.

A walk to the livery stable would provide his main exercise for the evening. Aboard Lincoln he headed to the part of town where the rich and the wealthy spent their time employing maids and governesses as Prescott grew in size and stature.

While the rowdy days of the Wild West weren't totally gone from Prescott, there was a growing upper crust and a burgeoning middle class. Homes and schools were helping the dozens of churches fill every Sunday. The bars and saloons were just as busy as ever, but fewer gunshots were heard on a daily basis. Saturday night hadn't changed much, and women and children didn't spend Saturday nights in town anyway.

Lancer rode up to the Paulson house where the gas lamps were flickering and all seemed quiet. It was a nice night as he watched the sun set in the west over California. There was a slight chill in the air, but his warm coat was just right for evening fare. Once at the door, he was surprised to see Sarah Jane opening it.

"Where is Elmira this evening?" He questioned.

"She has the night off," Sarah Jane explained calmly. "Although I made sure she cooked a grand meal for us before she went off to see her daughter. Her daughter is newly a mother and Elmira just can't bear to leave her alone. She's been making the trip to Cottonwood often."

Lancer entered at Sarah Jane's insistence. She took his hat and offered to take his coat but with his shoulder holster covered he chose to keep it on.

"A gentleman prefers to keep his coat if he's going to be alone with a lady," he suggested, as she blushed. "We are going to be alone are we not?"

"Yes Mr. Lancer, Miley is out for the night," she responded. "She's out with her granddaughter this evening."

"Wilamena?"

The utterance of her name very much surprised the woman.

"I ran into her the other day," Lancer responded with a cool notion, not missing a beat. "Nice young girl."

Lancer waited to see Sarah Jane's response, which she kept it to herself. In fact, she didn't even acknowledge it. A fact Lancer found interesting. She motioned for him to sit and she brought out a tray with two glasses of wine.

"I hope you like Chianti, Lancer," she offered up. "It's from my own vineyards near Cottonwood."

Lancer took the glass and swirled it. He raised it to his nostrils and let the aroma engage his instincts before lowering his head into the glass and taking the first sip.

"You are a connoisseur of many things," Sarah Jane said with respect.

"Give me a bowl of wine, in this I bury all un-kindness," Lancer said as he raised his glass high to the ceiling.

"Bravo!" She answered. "Shakespeare?"

"Julius Caesar," he replied fondly.

"I've always loved the Bard," Sarah Jane spoke highly. "He was such a cultural genius."

Lancer took another sip before tossing it back to Sarah Jane.

"His genius is that he wrote for the masses, the little people and the poor," Lancer responded, looking upon his hostess firmly.

Sarah Jane took it as the poignant insult it was meant to be. She felt immediately uncomfortable and yet she tried to play along. She knew little of Shakespeare except what her own husband had taught her and her comments allowed Lancer to see her true inner self. She had been putting on airs more than he had expected. Now he knew she was certainly capable of the crime he suspected her of. This was going to be an interesting evening.

"Shall we move to the dining room?"

It was her quick way out of an uncomfortable situation.

He followed behind, being led by the hostess who was at least gracious, if not worldly wise.

"May I help you?" He asked.

She informed him she was capable of serving the meal. She wasn't in the kitchen but a moment and returned with roast chicken on a platter with red potatoes and corn. Alongside were steaming hot dinner rolls in a basket.

"Oh I almost forgot the piece de resistance," she uttered in a quick high tone, making sure Lancer at least heard her perfect French pronunciation. "The quiche is Elmira's specialty."

Sarah Jane returned just as quickly with the beautifully done Quiche Loraine.

"Ah one of my favorites, you will have to pass along my praise to Elmira when she returns," Lancer said, licking his lips. "I've always been fond of Quiche Loraine."

Sarah Jane smiled broadly. She had come back from the insult. While she felt like laying one on of her own, she wasn't up to Lancer's worldly wit just yet. She thought to herself before the night was over, she would make that move; for now, enjoy the meal. For his part Lancer felt one insult was enough for the night. He knew while the dish being served was French, quiche itself was of German origination. He let it go.

Sarah Jane sat down across the table from her guest who couldn't help but take in the compilation of wonderful smells his pallet was waiting to taste. He could feel the slight groan in the pit of his stomach as he ached for what lay before him. He knew Elmira was a good cook; however the aroma filling the room let him know she was a great cook.

Dinner conversation was mainly chit chat. Neither Lancer nor his host wanted to disrupt the taste, the wine or the company with business. Sarah Jane did try to pry as much out of Lancer as she could. She began by prompting him to discuss his background.

"I know you were in the war, Mr. Lancer, and I know you fought for the union but I don't know much about your background other than that," Sarah Jane said coyly, as if she was seriously interested in the man's family history.

"There isn't much to tell, or that I care to tell, may be more like it," he said in a polite but private tone. "My war record stands for itself and after the war I moved west."

Sarah Jane paused for a moment to sip from her nearly empty glass. Lancer leaned forward to refill the goblet. Her eyes could not help but see the politeness of the man. He was obviously educated. He certainly must be well traveled too.

"Is the West to your liking?"

"It suits me for the moment."

"Why the gun?"

Lancer wiped his mouth with the cloth napkin and leaned back. He knew there were some things his employer had the right to know and there were other things he had just as much right to hold back.

"I like helping people Sarah, it gives me sense of purpose and I like helping those who need help more than those who want to topple someone else due to greed or anger," he said, in a straightforward manner.

"And your fee?"

"A man has to eat, and while I don't need the money as much as some men do, I find if a relationship has some business aspect to it, it usually works out better for everyone involved."

"And those marks on your holster, which I see you are not carrying this evening," she said with a smile.

"The crossed lances?" He halted before speaking, raising his head to the heavens. "Lances were the tools of a medieval warrior on horseback. The Knights Templar used swords, archers used arrows and the heavy horse was the tool used to scare an army into quickly turning tail and running. The Lance, uh the noble Lancer, used his weapon from a distance while always moving forward. You see, Sarah Jane, when a soldier on horseback carried a lance he had no choice but to keep moving forward. If he turned to the side, someone else would get hurt; if he stopped he'd get someone else's lance in the back. His mission was to always press on until the job or he himself was finished."

Sarah Jane marveled at the man's intellect as he told his story. Lancer took a last sip of the tasty wine she provided and looked at his host to see her reaction. It seemed he had captivated her to the point she was speechless. If only for a moment since Sarah Jane Paulson's mind was always working overtime.

"Shall we take our dessert in the parlor?"

Lancer nodded as he rose and started to take his plate from the table.

"Oh no, Mr. Lancer, you are a guest in my home and Elmira will return in the morning to clear the dishes," she said with a high-handed tone. "That's her job, not mine, and certainly not that of my guest."

He dipped his head, grabbed the wine bottle and his glass and moved to the parlor, where he sat facing the mantle. He noticed the photo of the Oxford Rowing team was no longer in sight. His mind began to wander but not for long. Sarah Jane returned with two plates on a tray alongside a coffee pot and two cups.

"Fresh strawberries, sweet cream and what looks to be a light and airy English biscuit," Lancer noted. "Am I correct in my assumption?"

"You are sir," she answered. "I do love these biscuits. I have them imported along with chutney and a few other foreign delicacies. Not unlike your Turkish Delight."

He didn't look up at the suggestion but Lancer knew she had done her own research. She was a smart woman but hopefully she did not find out about his taste for the soft treat from Molly. That would be unfortunate.

"I do love some of the things you can only get in Europe," he answered. "There is a wonderful pastry shop near the center of Paris which has the most delectable soft cookie. On the outside it has a sweet, but not too sweet icing, but inside is a mascarpone style sweet cheese which will send your taste buds to the moon. I do miss those things every once in a while."

"It sounds like heaven," she swooned with a laugh. "It must be difficult living in Tombstone when there is a huge world you've been to already."

He swirled the cream and berries in his mouth, absorbing the entire flavor before answering.

"Tombstone has a growing society now with the arts, opera and high quality talent coming in," he bragged. "The silver strikes have brought a more diverse clientele."

"Ah yes, the more money the better class of people you get, won't you agree?"

The comments were difficult for Lancer to swallow. He'd always been on the top of the financial scale and hated what money did to most people.

"It all depends on the people," he started out. "Money sometimes brings out the worst in people and often brings in the worst people period. I do not envy those who fall into money and have no idea how to handle their new-found good fortune. Tombstone is full of those. Even my friends the Earp's have had their financial ups and downs."

Sarah Jane listened intently, leaning forward at the mention of the famous Earp brothers.

"You know Wyatt Earp?"

"Had a meeting with him just before I left."

"And his brother? Virgil?"

"Your former lawman here in Prescott."

Sarah Jane became discontent with the conversation when it turned to Virgil Earp. Lancer could not help seeing the irony.

"You know him?"

"Only by reputation," she answered. "Nothing else."

Sarah Jane recomposed herself and smiled sweetly at the man in front of her. She had invited him to her home for a reason. It was her request and he had not yet asked why. It puzzled her so she decided to make the first move. She got up off her seat and moved over next to him on the love seat. Lancer did not resist. He did not reposition himself right away but sat straight forward on the seat.

"Do you wonder why I asked you here tonight?"

"It had occurred to me, but I figured we'd get to that in due time."

Sarah Jane looked up at Lancer now with wanting eyes. She stared at his curly hair wrapped around his ears. He was a handsome man and she had not been with a mature man like him in a long time. For all his youth and strength, Landry Smith, was not mature. Even when she had such maturity it was with Henry, and the last few years of their relationship were almost lifeless. If indeed the relationship had any life to it at all.

Sarah Jane reached out her finger and touched the curled hair which circled his left ear. She wound her finger with it and then stroked his ear. Lancer could feel the sensuousness of the woman as she touched him. He slowly turned toward her. As he looked into her eyes he spoke softly.

"This isn't the normal relationship between an employer and an employee, Mrs. Paulson."

"When the boss wants something from their employee, they usually get it or the employee loses their job," she said softly not looking into his eyes but staring at his hair as she twirled the curls even more. "And since I've paid you your fee, you owe me until the job is done and whatever falls in between."

Lancer could not help but be attracted to her. She was beautiful, warm, cunning and yet just a little bit dangerous. She was the perfect mix of delicate, sexy and the kind of woman your father warned you about. Danger lurked within her but outside she drew men into a web which some men could not get free of.

Lancer looked at her deeply and leaned in to kiss her waiting lips. They locked lips as her red lipstick transferred slightly to his mouth. When she finished the kiss she placed her red lips on his collar, leaving a slight mark on his white shirt. As he held her tightly she suddenly pushed him away and while holding onto his arm with her right arm, she reached over and tore the top part of her dress with her left hand. It left her breast nearly exposed and as fake anguish shown on her face and shock was displayed on his, she screamed.

"No!" She yelled loudly, "No, no stop! Unhand me you brute!"

Lancer tried to calm her down trying to figure out what just happened.

"Sarah what the…"

Just then he heard the front door burst open and Deputy Landry Smith bolted in with his gun at the ready; cocked and pointed at Lancer. Suddenly Lancer knew he had been duped into the oldest con in the book.

"Put your hands up Lancer, hold 'em high!" Smith shouted standing just a few feet away from the gunman.

Lancer did what he was told. He understood fully the deputy was just waiting for him to reach for his gun. Or, to try something to disrupt the situation so he could plug the gunman, no questions asked. Lancer's arms were held high as Sarah Jane rushed to the deputy's side.

"Oh deputy, it was awful, he tried to rape me," she cried. "Look he tore my dress, he said awful things to me, and if you hadn't come in just then, well, I don't know what would have happened."

"There, there now missy," he pretended not to know her personally. "I got him now; he won't be bothering you anymore."

Lancer sat with his hands held in the air. Smith stood behind him and cuffed those hands together behind Lancer's back.

"One wrong move mister and I'll plug you where you stand," Smith warned Lancer. "We respect our women out here, and it would give me great pleasure to fill you full of lead."

Lancer got up slowly, hands behind his back as Smith searched him for a weapon. He pulled the .22 pistol from his shoulder holster and showed it to Sarah Jane. Looking angry she walked over and slapped him across the face. Lancer's demeanor barely moved.

"You pig, you'll get yours."

"Oh knock off the act Mrs. Paulson, we all know the score here," Lancer said sternly. "You set me up because I was getting too close to finding out who killed your husband; you and your lover here, Mr. Landry Smith. Now you want to kill me to make it look like I'm the bad guy from out of town."

"And it worked," Smith said proudly looking at Lancer.

"Shut up Landry," Sarah Jane, now in full control, angrily snapped at Smith.

"What I still can't figure out is the connection between you and Lovling and the mine," Lancer spoke up. "What do you have on him that kept him from advancing in politics?"

Smith knew Lancer had figured out most of what happened. Confident he had the man in black exactly where he wanted him, he spoke out confidently. Sarah Jane was not amused.

"It is a matter of reputation when an illegitimate son returns from the past to haunt your future," Smith started to reveal.

"I said shut up, I'm through with you Landry," Sarah Jane snapped again. "He knows enough already and I won't be satisfied until he's out of the picture."

Smith was not amused. He was losing his control of the situation to his female partner and he wasn't happy about it. Lancer sensed it quickly and decided to keep talking to try to turn the two of them against each other.

"You didn't see this coming did you Landry?" He said with slyness in his voice. "Taking out Henry Paulson was easy. An accidental explosion in a mine, the body buried under tons of rock and no evidence. You get the girl and the money. This is different though. This is premeditated murder. You'll hang for this one."

Landry was listening to what Lancer had to say and as he rubbed his chin Sarah Jane was smart enough to read Lancer's game. She quickly turned the tables again.

"Don't listen to him Landry, he's just trying to play us off each other," she pleaded sternly. "Don't you see what he's doing?"

"Maybe, but he makes sense, baby," Smith offered back.

Sarah Jane could take no more and ordered Lancer outside to the back of the house. As they approached the back door Lancer could see Smith had brought Lincoln around back during dinner. The gun at his back kept him from trying anything at the moment although he saw several possibilities. He knew he'd never make it back to the jail, but thought there might be an opportunity to make a break on the way.

"Let's see, will I or won't I make it back to the jail house?" He queried Smith. "I mean, you won't risk a trial. Too much information might come out. If I make it back to the jail and get shot while trying to escape you'd have to kill me or I might just be able to convince Sheriff Jackson you are not all you're cracked up to be. So it looks like I'll be shot while trying to escape on the way there. You have a history with that don't you? Bad idea."

"I said shut up Lancer!" Sarah Jane ripped.

"Mister, you talk too much," Smith chipped in.

Sarah Jane held the gun while Smith helped put Lancer on Lincoln. His hands were cuffed behind his back so the move was difficult. Lincoln was a great horse and the man and the horse usually operated as one. Lancer would wait his opportunity.

"If you are going to shoot me while I am trying to escape you probably should take the cuffs off me, Landry, because it won't work," Lancer said calmly.

"And why not?" The deputy asked sarcastically.

Lancer adjusted himself on the saddle as he prepared to speak.

"Simply because if I die with my hands cuffed behind me no one will believe you had to shoot me in the back, so if you are going to leave me in handcuffs then they should be in front where I would have some wiggle room," he pointed out. "No one is going to give you the benefit of the doubt for shooting a man in the back while his hands are cuffed behind him."

Sarah Jane didn't budge but Smith thought about it for a moment. Lancer seized the opportunity to expound on the matter. He knew Landry Smith was not an educated man and if he could spread some doubt over the situation it might just help his cause.

"And besides if you shoot me and I die quickly with handcuffs on it will leave a sudden mark on my wrists which would indicate the blood traveling through my veins came more quickly to the surface also indicating my hands had previously been cuffed behind me," Lancer said with a hint of bull in his delivery. "In that case, and every experienced lawman, and certainly your county coroner of which you have a good one here in Prescott, again in that case, everyone will know that my hands were tied behind me, then tied again in front of me. Now sir, this just won't look good and will leave some doubt in the minds of the jury."

The comments left Smith totally perplexed as he looked up at Sarah Jane on her horse.

"What do you think?" He asked her. "Is he telling the truth?"

"It sounds good and as I've come to learn, Mister Lancer is an educated man," she pondered. "He is also an intelligent man, intelligent enough to spin a yarn well enough to make you think you need to undo his hands."

"Which would make it easier for me to escape," Lancer finished her sentence. "Now that, my dear Deputy Smith, is a question you have to ask yourself. Do you feel good enough about all of this to give me that one chance or do you take your chances with an experienced lawman, coroner and a jury of your peers, to make this whole thing go away?"

Smith left Lancer's hands bound behind his back as he mounted his horse but would not answer the man in black. Sarah Jane remained quiet as well. Smith took Lincoln by the reins and led the horse and horseman off down the alley with Sarah Jane Paulson trailing behind with the gun.

"Tell me one thing Sarah Jane," Lancer continued keeping the conversation going. "The fifty-thousand in cash, jewels and gold?"

"It was only ten-thousand but fifty-thousand made it sound like Henry ran off and left me destitute," Sarah Jane answered. "It worked."

"And that was the ten-thousand you paid to Ken Golder to keep him quiet?" Lancer pursued the questioning. "It was the money he invested in Henry's mine."

Sarah Jane could only marvel at the suggestion.

"Mister Lancer, it is going to be a real shame to kill a man who is so good at deducing the truth," Sarah Jane spoke. "You are so good at what you do. I don't know how I will sleep at night knowing you are no longer with us."

"I'm sure you'll manage Sarah," Lancer said sarcastically.

As they moved down the alley they got to the next street. A left turn meant back to town but a right turn left Lancer in unfamiliar territory. Much to his chagrin, they turned Lincoln to the right. It was uncharted territory for him and he knew he only had a few minutes to make a decision. When he asked where they were going, Smith answered they were heading back to the jail, but they were going the long way around.

Lancer surmised it was a trail further from town where a gunshot would be less likely heard. If he did escape, the pair would have more time to catch him before he got to someone else along the way.

"By the way deputy, you never did tell the rest of the story as to why this whole thing went down," Lancer asked. "I mean, I'd like to know before I die what went on and who you really are."

"I guess it won't hurt to tell you," Smith said as Sarah Jane rolled her eyes knowing this was a lost cause. "I am the illegitimate son of James Lovling, Esquire and when a man runs for high office, especially for governor, well, such a son might make it impossible given the potential scandal and all."

"So you blackmailed your father, joined in with Paulson on this mining deal and when Paulson got into debt because the mine was dry, you put the bite on your old man?"

"Something like that, but the lawyer wasn't forthcoming, although we did make him a partner in the mine and made sure we were covered if anything happened," Smith added. "Sort of an insurance policy."

"An insurance policy which you conveniently cashed in upon Paulson's death, but you forgot Sarah Jane wanted him dead as well and bringing her into the game seemed a bit more intriguing," Lancer offered. "Henry's philandering didn't sit well with your Sarah Jane now did it?"

Sarah Jane only grimaced with the thought of Henry Paulson's infidelities.

"And more financially profitable since Henry had an insurance policy made out to her as well," Smith added. "More money in the pot."

As Lancer looked around for a place to make a break he kept talking.

"And it only seemed natural you could blackmail Lovling out of his share," Lancer added.

"Enough talk," Sarah Jane shouted. "He's dead and you're going to be."

"There is only one thing I don't understand here," Lancer said trying to delay the inevitable. "Why bring me into it?"

"You were the wild card Mister Lancer," Sarah Jane chipped in. "If we hired you to find Henry and you couldn't, we could make the claim he was either dead or disappeared. With your reputation for success it only seemed to reason that if you couldn't solve this, we could put it to rest and in a year we could put Henry to rest. No muss, no fuss and we get on with our lives."

"But you underestimated me." Lancer quipped.

"We did," Sarah Jane came back. "Too bad too, you are one of the finest gentlemen I ever met and it's going to be a shame to waste all you brought to the world. You should not have done your job so well."

Smith stopped the horses when they came to a clearing where the deed was to be done. Lancer knew this was his last chance and playing on Sarah Jane's comments and the fact the pair had become somewhat distracted via the talk, he decided it was time.

"So how about it, are you going to undo my hands so you can complete your plan with everything falling into place or are you going to leave that one thing to chance and possibly screw it up for the both of you?" Lancer calmly placed his words.

Smith looked at Sarah Jane and shrugged. She lamented but held up her pistol and cocked it as she did. She meant business and with the business end of the gun pointing right at him, Lancer knew his calculations had to be perfect.

Smith walked up to Lincoln, pulled out his key and dutifully opened the handcuffs. Lancer rubbed his hands over his wrists feeling the freedom he hadn't felt for about an hour. He reached down and took the reins of his powerful steed and looked back at Sarah Jane, calculating the angle of the gun as he sat there.

"Now move on Mr. Lancer, just a few feet so I can plug you right," she said as she held the gun higher.

This was Lancer's chance. As soon as he saw the gun elevate he kicked Lincoln hard. When the mighty horse charged forward the rider rolled to the left side of his saddle with Lincoln shielding him from the discharge of Sarah Jane's weapon. The shot sailed well over his outstretched body and into the woods nearby. As the horse picked up speed, Smith reached for his weapon and fired again coming nowhere close to the horse and rider speeding away.

"After him, don't let him get away!" Sarah Jane yelled, as Smith mounted his horse which was behind the quickly moving female rider at this point.

Lancer rode Lincoln as fast as he could, opening up good distance between them. He didn't know the trail but he took it where the road took him, dashing and darting while looking for a place which possibly might provide cover. A stream bed lay ahead and the road crossed through it. The great horse moved across it like the biblical walking on water. He was over the stream in two strides while the killers were racing hard behind him.

Lancer could see mountains off to his left and Prescott in a distance off to his right. If he raced back to Prescott he'd have to find the sheriff quickly and convince him his deputy was a killer and a criminal. He understood that would take time and time was something he didn't have. He might get a bullet in the back as soon as he got into town. Gunfire might erupt; innocent bystanders might get in the way. No, Prescott proper was out.

Lancer veered Lincoln to the left trail at a fork in the road. He would head for the mountains and hopefully make a stand. He didn't have a hand gun except for the two-shot derringer he kept in his belt. Smith had not found that. He had a sawed off shotgun in his saddle bag, which Smith did not deem important enough to search. For that he needed close range which was not something he was counting on.

"Ride you son of a bitch, ride," Sarah Jane, now in full anger mode shouted to Smith. "Don't let him get away."

As they came to the fork in the road they stopped, wondering which way the rider had gone. They reasoned for a moment whether they should go toward the mountains or town.

"If he went to town we'll get him there, we still have the escape angle and it will take some convincing to allow him to get his story across," Sarah Jane explained.

"And if he went into the mountains it's to our advantage," Smith offered back. "We can get a lynch mob up and go after him, or at least a posse."

They turned their horses and moved toward Prescott only about five minutes ride away.

Lancer made the hills and didn't see any dust behind him. He quickly realized what had happened. He was a fugitive. Smith and Sarah Jane were heading to town to tell their story and soon, probably around daybreak, a posse would make its way into the hills. Word would be all over town and no one was going to believe him; not John Henry, not Cleveland Grover and certainly not Sheriff Jackson. The only person who might believe him was a 13 year old girl named Willie. She was his only chance and he didn't want to involve her. He didn't have much choice to clear his name and bring justice to this case.

Upon reaching the base of the mountain he saw a small cave. Large enough for a man to sleep and make a small fire. This would be his hiding place. He still had some food in Lincoln's saddle bags and coffee was going to taste real good in a few minutes. First, though, he needed to trust Lincoln to take a message to Willie.

He emptied his saddle bags and wrote a note to
Willie explaining briefly what happened. He
needed her help and she should follow Lincoln
back to his hide out. His guns were in his room
and she'd have to find a way to get into the room
and bring them along. Lancer knew she was re-
sourceful and sent Lincoln on his way.

CHAPTER SEVENTEEN

Sheriff Jackson couldn't believe his ears when Smith and Sarah Jane explained what happened.

"I don't want to believe it," Jackson pleaded. "Not with his reputation."

"Sheriff, look at my dress, he ripped it right off my body and if Landry here hadn't been patrolling the street and heard my screams, who knows what might have happened to me," she cried. "I hate to think of what might be happening to other women, defenseless women."

The sheriff had no choice but to believe them and round up a posse. He sent Smith out to the Long Branch, the Palace and the Prescott hotels to get some men.

"Get good men, local men, we don't want a lynch mob," Jackson told Smith, who nodded.

Sarah Jane sat down and had a drink offered by the sheriff to help her calm down. Smith made his way to the Long Branch.

"Everyone listen up," he yelled, upon entering the door of the big saloon. "We got trouble. Sarah Jane Paulson was brutally attacked and near raped by that hired killer lurking in our town. It's Lancer. You've all heard his name and his reputation. He's holed up in the hills north of town and we're forming a posse to go get that mangy beast and raper of women! Who's with me?!"

A dozen men yelled angrily as they grabbed their guns and immediately followed Smith, moving on to the next saloon. The same scenario played out there and soon 40 guns were waiting outside the jail house for Sheriff Jackson to come out. When he did he was shocked and angered. He looked at his deputy with disdain as the anxious men chimed in. One threw a rope onto the porch in front of the jail as a sign Jackson knew all too well.

"Now you men go home, I don't need forty guns and I certainly don't need a rope," Jackson said, trying to calm them down.

"We're here to see justice is done!" Shouted one of them.

"At the end of a rope!" Yelled another.

Smith stood by not offering a hand one way or the other, knowing the sheriff was no match for this. He knew the men were angry enough to take matters into their own hands.

"We're not vigilante's, I want a posse of responsible men," Jackson again pleaded. "Who is with me?"

No one budged and even Jackson had to concede he was not going to handle an unruly crowd bent on vengeance. He would try once again but it would be his undoing.

"Now I'm telling you, you men go home," he tried to convince them once again. "We're going to bring this man back to stand trial. It is…"

Jackson could barely get the words out of his mouth when a rock from the crowd hit him square in the forehead knocking him unconscious. Smith jumped off his horse and raced to his side. He motioned for two men to take him into the jailhouse where he could recover.

"You call Doc Haver," Smith shouted to one man. "Now, let's get this Lancer. C'mon men, it's time to act."

With that Smith jumped on his horse and led the entire party out of town at breakneck speed. Not a man in the crowd was convinced there need be a trial. This was vengeance. One of their own women, a high class woman any of them would be proud to call his own, had been raped by an out-of-town hired gun. They would have their revenge.

Inside their tiny little home Willie and her mother Lilly were having supper when Lincoln ponied up in front. The hard neighing of the black stallion could be heard for 50 yards and Willie was the first to respond.

"Momma, its Mr. Lancer's horse," she yelled as she ran to see what was the matter. "Something's wrong."

The two of them raced outside and Willie quickly spotted a note tied to Lincoln's saddle horn. It explained the situation, and her mother agreed this was urgent.

"We need to get to the sheriff," her mother explained.

"You go there and I'll meet you shortly," Willie instructed her mother. "I've got to do something first."

Before she could object to her daughter's choice, Willie was astride Lincoln and off down the road. Lilly kept the note, mounted her own horse and headed to town. She would meet Willie at the jail-house and hoped it wouldn't be too late.

Lancer made a small fire. He figured he had some time, so food and coffee were necessary elements to his survival. It might be days before they found him; then again it might be hours. He was willing to take that chance. He checked his weapons and figured he could hold off a few men for a few hours. If they came in force or decided to wait him out, he was good as dead.

Willie crept up the back steps to the Palace Hotel and snuck in. She knew Lancer's room and stole down the hallway hoping no one would notice. She was in luck, no one did. She tried the door but it was locked and there was no way the clerk was going to give her the key. She heard one of the dance hall girls and a man coming around the bend and she ducked into a darkly lit portion of the hallway. She quickly dimmed the gas lamp nearby, covering her in darkness.

As she heard the rowdy couple enter a room down the hall, she knew she had to work fast and ran right up to the room again. She reached into her pocket for her small knife and slipped it into the door lock. A few jiggers later she heard the door pop and went inside. There on the bed lay the gun belt with the crossed lances. She hurriedly grabbed it and made her way back down the stairs to the waiting Lincoln. With swiftness only a young teen could muster she rode the stallion to the jailhouse where her mother waited inside.

As she entered, the anticipation was growing. Lilly had shown the note to Sheriff Jackson who, to his credit grasped the situation just as Lancer had hoped he would. Jackson had recovered quickly with the help of Doc Haver and was ready to take charge.

"Little girl, you have done a great deed and possibly saved a man's life in the process, now give me that gun and stay here with your mother 'til we come back," Jackson ordered.

Willie was angered at the suggestion and pulled the gun belt behind her. She was not about to miss out on this. Mr. Lancer had sent for her and she was not going to let him down.

"Willie, give the sheriff the gun," Lilly pleaded as only a mother could.

"No, Mr. Lancer sent for me and I'm going whether you like it or not," she snapped back.

When Jackson moved toward her she bolted out the door. In one swift motion Willie leaped upon Lincoln who instinctively took off, with the rider holding on for dear life. Down the road he sped with an anxious and confident Willie on board like a race horse and jockey.

Jackson and Lilly knew there was no stopping her and they had no choice but to follow. Jackson would have preferred Lilly stay behind but he knew she was as headstrong as her daughter. She was going and not one was stopping her.

Willie rode Lincoln hard. Jackson and Lilly were right behind. Willie couldn't chance they would catch her and send her back to town so she rode as fast as Lincoln would travel. It was only about three miles outside of town to where Lancer was hiding out but Willie could see the glow of the torchlights in the distance. She knew the mob was there ahead of her and she needed to get close enough to see if they had taken Lancer, dead or alive.

She pulled up about 20 yards short of the camp-fires lit by the mob. She could see she was still in time. They had settled in for the night. She surveyed the situation and heard them talking. They were sure Lancer was in the hills and probably in a cave. There were lots of caves but which one they were not sure. It could mean a life or two if they picked the wrong one. They chose to wait until daybreak to move forward. This was welcome news to Willie.

Her mother and the sheriff came up behind her. Willie was relieved to see they were there to help and not to send her back. Jackson realized what was happening and also realized since the mob was going to wait until daybreak so would he. After a lousy night's sleep on the cold ground they might be a little more apt to listen to him. Right now they were a mob. Time would help.

While they weren't happy about it, they knew their best chance was to let Willie move around behind the campfires with Lincoln and take Lancer what he asked for. He would be expecting Willie riding on Lincoln. Someone else might get shot. No one wanted to take chances, so the girl seemed the best bet.

With Willie having left the site, Jackson could hear Smith giving orders to the others. He had riled them up for a cause and for some reason wanted Lancer dead. If there was a crime committed, he thought, Lancer would be brought to stand trial. If not, and it looked like that was a distinct possibility, he had a corrupt deputy to deal with.

As Willie led Lincoln up into the rocks she could see a small flicker from a cave. It was hidden from where the mob was staging camp. The entrance was off to the side. While some caves would shine their lighted fires off other rocks and the glow could be seen for miles, Lancer knew better and selected one which could not be seen. Willie saw it when she moved in and tried to get his attention. She tossed a rock into the cave and he jumped up. He moved cautiously to the entrance.

"Mr. Lancer," she whispered. "It's me, Willie."

Relieved, Lancer moved to the front of the cave and invited her in. She tied up Lincoln nearby and brought the gun in with her. He hugged her close to his chest. She smiled and then gave him some food wrapped up in a small towel.

"My mom's corn pone and some jerky," she said. "I thought you might be hungry."

Sitting down, Lancer savored the food and he just as quickly devoured it. The adrenaline pumping through his body had eaten up anything he had from dinner. He was indeed hungry and was glad the young lady had thought about his welfare. He strapped on his gun and told Willie she had to leave. She convinced him to let her stay for a while. The posse was not coming until day-break.

The minutes turned to hours, and Willie fell asleep in his arms. He looked upon her knowing what a special girl she was and what an even more special woman she would grow up to be. It would be light soon and he woke her to make her leave.

"I'm not leaving you alone, Lancer. I'm staying and you can't make me go," she said sternly before lowering her head. "Even if you spank me, I'm not leaving."

He knew there was no pleading with the little girl. He had to make her understand she was in grave danger and by staying was endangering his life as well. She would not hear of it.

"Look you little baby, I don't need you here, I don't want you here, and what I need for you is to go and leave me alone," he pleaded even against his own heart. "Now get out of here! Go home and play with your dolls."

The words pierced her very soul. They were hurtful and made her angry. The combination of the two feelings forced tears to roll down her cheeks.

"I hate you, I hate you, I hope they gun you down for what you did to my Aunt Sarah," she screamed. "You used me."

Even though she said the words she knew they were not true. For Lancer those cutting words were almost more than he could bear. He tried to convince her to leave by lying to her and the words he was hearing back stung harder than a bee. He knew, though, she had to leave. If the shooting started she would be in the way and even as he was dying he would regret even more the loss of this young, precious girl.

Even as she started to leave, she tried hard to stay. Willie was strong, and while she said the words and heard Lancer's words, she didn't want to believe them. Perhaps in her own way she knew what he was doing and she had to leave. When she got to the front of the cave the darkness was beginning to lift. She had to make her way back down the hill and maybe this was going to be the last time she saw this man.

Suddenly she turned and ran to him. She threw her arms around him hugging him for dear life. Holding on and never wanting to let go.

"Don't send me away, I love you Lancer, I love you," she cried, tears streaming down her face.

His tears held back even though they were gushing from within. He held on and didn't say a word. He let her hold on until she could hold no longer. Lancer looked down, kissed her on the forehead and she knew she had to go. He smiled as she did and as she crossed the threshold of the cave and walked out of sight he broke down and fell to his knees. There in a crumpled mess he thought about what his life had become. What would he do if he survived? It wasn't likely but it was a question he was not prepared to answer.

Lilly and Jackson kept a close watch on the men in the posse. Soon things became quiet. They were bedding down for the night and even Smith was quiet. Jackson convinced Lilly to get some sleep and they took turns watching over the camp. As daybreak was nearing they heard a rider coming slowly. Jackson turned to see Lovling coming toward them. He looked like a man who wanted to talk.

When he dismounted he looked over the scene and motioned to Sheriff Jackson he needed to talk with him. Jackson left Lilly to keep an eye on things while he went a safe distance away. Voices carry in the wild and he didn't want to give away his position.

"I know what's happening here sheriff and I suppose it's partly my fault," Lovling began. "Deputy Landry Smith is actually my son. I knew his mother, a young girl whom I should have never been with, but sometimes a man can only be a man."

Jackson wasn't too pleased. He was even angrier when he learned from Lovling the young girl was no older than Willie, when she delivered Smith. She died in childbirth, making the words Lovling spoke even more pathetic and tragic.

"You're scum, Lovling, pure scum, and now this," Jackson uttered in anger.

Lovling could only lower his head in shame. He went on to tell Jackson about how Smith had blackmailed him over his politics and then got him mixed up with the mine and Paulson. When Paulson started gambling heavily he got into heavy debt. He had already taken refuge with one of the dance hall girls in town and when Sarah Jane found out about it she was furious. She and Landry cooked up a scheme to get rid of Henry Paulson by trapping him in the mine and blowing it up. They hoped to make it look like an accident if anyone ever did find out.

"So for Sarah Jane it was revenge?"

"As well as money," the lawyer answered. "Henry was well-insured and when Landry figured he could collect on the insurance from Henry's death in the mine and tie in with Sarah Jane, it all fell into place."

"Until Lancer arrived and started digging?"

"Yes," the lawyer answered. "The nitro on the dead man's pants was a dead giveaway. He was one of the two men who ambushed the two of you. The other was Billy Tuesday. He's out there now I suppose with Landry."

Knowing what he knew now, the sheriff had to come up with a plan to turn the mob on Landry Smith. This wasn't going to be easy. He'd seen the man called Billy Tuesday before. He was in the mob and was a killer who would not be taken.

They went back to the spot where they left Lilly, who was in a panic when they arrived.

"Sheriff, Smith and another man left a few minutes ago on their own for the caves," Lilly said fearfully. "Willie isn't back yet."

"They've gone to get Lancer on their own," Lovling offered.

Willie was about fifty yards away from the cave where she left Lancer, when suddenly a large hand covered her mouth from behind and another grabbed her around the waste.

"Well, looky here, we got us a hostage," Billy Tuesday said, with a sneering grin. "Pretty little thing too, ain't she?"

"Where is he?" Smith growled.

Willie would only shake her head as she tried vainly to get out of Tuesday's grip. She was not going to tell and Smith knew it. The anger welled up inside him and he struck her across the face with the flat of his hand.

"Now don't hurt her none, deputy," Tuesday pleaded with a grin. "Don't damage these pretty little goods. I might want to have some fun later on when this is over."

"There won't be any later," Lancer said in a stern voice, his pistol pointed right at Tuesday. "Now let her go. It's me you want."

Tuesday grinned ever bigger as he held his gun to Willie's head. Her eyes wide open and seeing the fear in those eyes, Lancer could not budge. He couldn't take the chance and Willie knew it.

"Well look at this, the gunslinger wants her all to hisself," Tuesday snarled. "Bet he's taken liberty already. How's it taste Mr. Gunslinger, a young one like…"

At that very moment Willie sunk her pearly white teeth deep into Tuesday's hand. As the gunman screamed she pulled away but not before Smith could take her into the same position and put a gun to her head.

It wasn't so fortunate for Tuesday for as quickly as he let Willie go the blazing speed of Lancer's gun placed two shots dead center into Tuesday's chest. When he fell back Lancer turned his weapon toward Smith but realized he was in the same situation, just one less man to face.

"Go ahead Lancer, take your best shot and I guarantee I'll put a bullet right through her pretty little head. Do it!" Smith yelled in a maniacal tone. "Put it down Lancer, put it down."

Lancer had little choice even as Willie shook her head no.

Down below, the gun shot rang through the valley and the mob was awakened. They stirred and started to move but Sheriff Jackson, both guns drawn quickly moved to meet them. Alongside him stood Lilly with a shotgun lowered to meet the first man who flinched.

"Stay right there men," Jackson ordered. "I'll plug the first one who moves and Lilly here will aim just a little lower. She can make a lot of geldings here this morning with that scatter gun."

The men all raised their hands and on the orders of the sheriff dropped their gun belts. Unbeknownst to Jackson who was explaining the situation to the posse, Lovling slipped away and headed toward the caves.

"All right now, deputy, you've won, I'm putting my gun down, now let her go," Lancer said bending down slowly to lay his gun on the ground. "You be careful with that, you only have an accessory to murder on your hands now. If you let that trigger slip, it's the hangman's noose for you. Don't let Sarah Jane get away with this."

"I love her, I love her," Smith whined as he cocked the gun pointed at Willie's head. "I know she used me, but I love her."

Lancer tried to figure out the words to get him to ease off but they weren't coming. Just then the right words seemed to be coming from behind Smith.

"Son, we all love someone," Lovling said, as he slowly approached.

Smith turned quickly but was still able to keep Lancer in his sights.

"I know you're hurting, Landry, and I've not been a good father to you, hell, I've never even been a father to you," Lovling pleaded.

"Father? You've been everything but," Smith turned toward him a bit more. "I hate your guts. Did you even love my mother?"

Willie slowly felt Smith's grip loosening and eyed Lancer. He could see her mind moving to get away, to give him an opportunity.

"I met your mother and I can't say I ever loved…"

Suddenly Smith fired a deft shot into Lovling's forehead right between his eyes. While he turned Willie broke away. Lancer dove to the ground, grabbed his pistol and fired two shots into Smith's chest as he spun around. Smith's body fell lifeless to the ground, rolled down the hill and into the gully below. Watching his body fall, tears of joy mixed with tears of pain rolled down Willie's cheeks. Willie rushed into Lancer's waiting arms.

She fell to her knees and buried her head in his chest, holding on for dear life. She had seen more death in two hours than most people see in a life-time. Death to the people she only knew from a distance and near-death to a man she would never forget. Her tears might wash away over the years but her memories of this moment would only fade slightly. In her older years they would grow fond-er, more memorable perhaps.

Sheriff Jackson and Lilly came running up the hill. Lilly ran to her daughter and fell to her knees to hug the little girl she bore. Lancer rose to meet Jackson. They looked down the hill at Smith's body lying in a heap. Jackson spied Lovling dead on the ground.

"He got what he deserved," Jackson said pointing to Lovling's body. "The sins of the father visited upon their children."

"The sins of the father visited on the son, sheriff?" Lancer said philosophically. "No. The fathers shall not be put to death for their children, neither shall the children be put to death for their fathers; every man shall be put to death for their own sins; Deuteronomy 24."

The sheriff shrugged and surveyed the situation once more.

"Billy Tuesday," he pointed out. "The other gunman who ambushed us that day."

"And Sarah Jane?" Lancer asked. "What becomes of her?"

"She'll stand trial for the murder of her husband," he said with a questioned look on his face. "Although I'm not sure we're going to get a conviction without a body. I guess we'll have to get that army you spoke of to open that mine back up. I'm sure we'll find the body of Henry Paulson."

Lancer pointed to the forty men down below. The sheriff smiled acknowledging the army existed.

"And I gather if you open that mine back up you will find the body of one Henry Paulson and probably Billy Joe Miller and maybe Mitchell Gatt," Lancer responded. "Seems Gatt disappeared about the same time as Paulson.

"You think he was in on it?" Sheriff Jackson asked.

"Seems plausible," Lancer surmised. "Gatt, Tuesday and Thornton. That's a lot of folks to keep something like this quiet and just too many folks to split up a pile of money. Someone got greedy. But sheriff, I'd just as soon see you keep that mine closed. It's been a bad omen for this town, a bad omen. And this town doesn't need another bad omen."

"You may be right, Mr. Lancer," Sheriff Jackson said. "I'll have to talk to the judge about that. Right now we got a heap of burying to do."

As the sheriff waved down to the posse to come up and deal with the bodies, Lancer walked arm in arm with Lilly and Willie down the mountain. Willie would grab Lincoln as they did, and the man in black hoisted her on top of the powerful horse. He'd done his job and Prescott was a much safer place than it was a couple weeks earlier.

EPILOUGE

For Willie and Lilly, their life would be much better. Sarah Jane was going to jail for a long time and the only one left to take care of her house and businesses was her mother, Miley. Miley of course was Willie's grandmother. Lilly, while never liked much by Miley, found new favor with her mother-in-law and the big house on the edge of Prescott was going to be a family place once again.

"Mr. Lancer, you come visit us again when you're up this way, will ya," Miley said, watching Lancer board Lincoln. "You're always welcome."

"I'll be sure I do as long as Elmira continues to make some of that wonderful strawberries and cream," Lancer said with a smile as he turned Lincoln toward the road.

"You can count on it!" Elmira yelled from the front porch.

Waving good-bye to each other everyone knew they'd likely never see Lancer again, but the adventure would never be forgotten.

Tombstone was bustling just like it was when he left. Wyatt Earp was still sitting at the Faro Table dealing cards, the Cowboys still ran their games, and cattle rustling remained a hot topic at the barber shop. For Lancer, a new adventure was just a newspaper story away.

"Mr. Lancer, I have a telegram for you," Javy said as he brought Lancer's breakfast. "It's from Los Angeles."

"Muchas gracias, Javier," Lancer replied, taking the telegram in one hand and sipping coffee with the other. "Los Angeles? Well let's see what the City of Angels has to offer these days."

OTHER BOOKS BY BOB BRILL:

Fan Letters to a Stripper; A Patti Waggin Tale is a coffee-table biography about real life burlesque queen, Patti Waggin and her Major League Baseball playing husband, Don Rudolph. 2009 Schiffer Books.

No Barrier; How the Internet Destroyed the World Economy, is a real world look at the Internet and what its inception has done to the world business model. One of the greatest inventions of all time, the World Wide Web also did a lot of damage to the economies of the world. 2012 Brill Productions.

Al Kabul; Home Grown Terrorist, is a novel set 25 years post 9-11. A special FBI team is charged with tracking down a home grow terrorist network which has designs on bringing down the government. This is a tale of greed, fanaticism and a hijacked religion. 2012 Brill Productions.

Due Soon:

Lancer; Hero of the West – The Los Angeles Affair.

All of the above books including this one are available on Amazon.com, through special ordering via bookstores and always at www.bobbrillbooks.com.